Anasazi Journey

James Gibson

Pentacles Press

This novel is a work of fiction. References to real people, events, establishments, and locales are intended only to give the fiction a sense of reality and authenticity. All of the main characters, organizations, events, and incidents in this novel are creations of the author's imagination, and their resemblance, if any, to actual persons, living or dead, or to organizations or events, is entirely coincidental.

Published by:
Pentacles Press
Subsidiary of James N. Gibson Enterprises, LLC.
340 N. Main Street, Suite 301B
Plymouth, MI 48167-8928
www.pentaclespress.com

In conjunction with:
Old Mountain Press, Inc.
2542 S. Edgewater Dr.
Fayetteville, NC 28303

www.oldmountainpress.com

Copyright © 2002 James N. Gibson Enterprises, LLC
Photo Mesa Verde copyright James Gibson
Digital photo work by Mark Gibson
ISBN: 0-9721351-0-3
Library of Congress Control Number: 2002107116

First Edition
Manufactured in the United States of America
1 2 3 4 5 6 7 8 9 10

Anasazi Journey

To Dick,
With Best Regards.

James N. Gibson
9 February 2005

In Memory of

Roald Einar Boen,
(April 21,1915 – May 8, 1998),

who introduced me to *There is a River: The Story of Edgar Cayce,* by Thomas Sugrue, and opened my mind to the possibilities.

Prologue

"The Lord our God said to us... 'You have stayed long enough at this mountain. Break camp and advance...'" (Deuteronomy 1:6, Bible, NIV)

❖

*T*he *shaman known as Tonah walked slowly to the edge of the promontory and gazed out to the horizon. His eyes swept across a vast land of lifeless desert and weathered hills. He turned to look down the canyon to his people, the Huastecs, huddled in misery in the noonday sun. They had been forced from their home in Mesa Verde and now they must find their ancestral home to the south. But the Huastecs were lost and they were suffering. If they did not find water and food soon, the people would begin dying. The burden was heavy upon Tonah, for as their leader, he must find the way.*

He sat down on the promontory, closed his eyes and slowed his breathing. He utilized his intention to alter the natural vibrations of his life force and moved his perception upward into the spirit world. He projected his awareness into the primordial chaos that was the potentiality of the evolving universe. Patterns of events that could be, or might never be, whirled in a maelstrom of color and light.

The desert and mountains reappeared in a reversed negative of the scene he had witnessed, and on the horizon he saw the black clouds of Death billowing and churning toward the Huastecs. In the clouds, he saw the shadows of other beings driving forward and felt their malevolence like a whiplash across his perception. Startled, he recoiled into the present and the lifeless desert reappeared.

Tonah shook his head with foreboding. He could not know where or how, but now he knew that Death was stalking the Huastecs. Soon Death would approach and he must find a way to overcome it.

MANCOS, COLORADO, WAS a sleepy town baking in the sun. A single street separated several weathered buildings, ending at the crude wooden bridge across the Mancos River, little more than a sluggish creek in late autumn.

A couple of horses stood hipshot at the hitching rail in front of the saloon. A dog trotted across the street toward the livery stable.

The sound of hooves rattled on the bridge as two riders appeared out of the dust. They dismounted at the hitching rail and entered through the sagging doors of the saloon.

"Whiskey," one of the men ordered without greeting. Rafe, the bartender, set up the drinks without expression. He saw that the men were trail worn. It was likely their dispositions would improve after they had their drinks. The riders tossed the drinks down and motioned for a refill. This time they sipped, savoring the drinks. One of the riders glanced up at Rafe.

"Always this quiet around here?"

"Mostly," Rafe answered genially. "The range hands stay out 'til Saturday night. Things get pretty lively then."

"Town could use some excitement, that's a fact. Say, we need supplies. Anybody handy who could outfit us?"

"There's a mercantile down the street. Storekeeper name of Odie runs it. He'll fix you up."

"Much obliged."

The rider flipped coins on the bar and turned. After nodding to his partner, they both walked out and swung into their saddles to ride the fifty yards or so to the general store.

Just like cowboys, Rafe thought, wouldn't walk ten feet as long as they could ride.

The men entered the cool interior of the store, noting the strong and familiar scent of leather goods and tobacco. The storekeeper was occupied with a customer and the men waited impatiently, hanging back in the shadows. Presently the customer completed her purchases and left the store.

"Odie?"

The storekeeper looked up, startled, as the riders strode toward him.

"Yes, that's me. What do you want, er...I mean, what can I do for you?"

"I'm Wilson, Tom Wilson, and this is my pard, Jake Long. The boss said to ask around, let on we didn't know you. Said you had a proposition for us."

"Your boss and I go back a ways. I asked him to send two trustworthy men. I guess that's you. Let's go in the back where we can talk."

Odie hurried to the front of the store, hung a sign out that he'd return shortly, and locked the door. With an air of mystery, he led the riders to the back room.

Odie's hands shook as he took down a locked box from which he removed a silver coin. He laid it on the desk in front of the men, watching them expectantly.

Wilson picked up the coin, looked it over and passed it to Long.

"Well, what do you think?" Odie prompted.

"It's old, damn old. What of it?"

"I'm certain that it's part of a lost Spanish silver shipment. I took a trip to Santa Fe after this turned up and looked up records. The Spaniards had silver mines somewhere northeast of here back in the 1700's. According to the records, an entire mule train of silver coins disappeared without a trace. Now this turns up. I believe there is a fortune lying near here, just waiting to be discovered and brought back."

Wilson's interest showed in his face.

"Where?"

"That's why you're here. I'll tell you what I know for half of what you find."

Wilson hedged. "It'll be risky. That's rough country."

"That's why I haven't gone after it myself. I know my limitations."

"Spill your story. If we decide to go, you'll get your half. If we don't, we ride out and no harm done."

"You should know that the man you work for is a friend of mine. He's guaranteed your word. If you double cross me, you've double crossed him."

Wilson looked up, his stare hard. "He told me as much. Now get on with your story!"

"All right, all right. No offense. We've got to understand each other. A couple of years ago, a man name of Stone was hanged by nightriders along the river. His son, Caleb, returned months later looking for revenge. He treed a big rancher name of Inman who was behind the hanging. Someone hired a gunman, Ben Slade, to take out Caleb, and he almost did, wounding him bad. Caleb managed to kill Slade for his trouble as he went down, then he holed up with some Indians in wild country south of here. When he returned, he was spending these. I think he found a cache of old Spanish treasure."

"How do you propose to start? You could ride that country 'til hell froze over and not find it."

"Caleb Stone rode out of here a week ago, heading south. Find him and make him take you to the treasure."

"Just like that?"

"Yep. Stone's tougher than he looks. That's why you men get half. You'll earn it."

Wilson glanced at Long, who whistled softly.

"We'll take the job." Wilson responded. "We'll need supplies."

"Tell me what you need, it's on the house, within reason, of course."

Wilson smiled. "Of course."

Later, Odie watched with satisfaction as Wilson and Long rode south, leading the heavily loaded packhorses.

FAR TO THE south in the hidden country of Mesa Verde a condor lifted on long wings, riding the air currents that swept up the canyons from the east. It rose higher, circling and searching the landscape far below. Presently its keen eyes detected the body of a man, stilled by death, leaning against a boulder at the bottom of a dry wash.

The condor descended, circling warily. Suddenly it became disoriented, rocking its wings to regain balance as it felt the awareness of Tonah, the shaman, touching its perception. A force of will overcame the condor, sending it into a powerful dive. It swooped down and grasped a large stone in its talons. It beat its wings, straining to lift the stone ever higher in the morning air. As the condor gained altitude, the awareness released the stone to plunge, gaining speed, to strike the boulders resting at the rim of the canyon.

The dislodged rock at the rim of the mesa began to slide, crashing into larger boulders. A low roar reverberated in the canyon as the avalanche crashed into the dry wash in a great cloud of dust. Silence returned as the dust blew away, leaving the body of the man forever buried beneath the debris.

The awareness of Tonah released the frightened condor and it sped away, seeking to escape the peril it did not understand.

Chapter 1

It was a vast, ancient land; a dry desert of graveled lowland and weathered mountains that stretched away to the horizon. The only movement was the heat that shimmered from the flats. It was a place where life clung to narrow niches and death came suddenly, leaving no mark upon the timeless face of the land.

A speck of life moved slowly between two serrated highlands, a mote insignificant on the flat canyon floor. Puffs of dust marked its passage and as it came closer, it became a horse and rider.

Caleb Stone paused to let the horse blow and wiped sweat in the oppressive heat. He scanned the surrounding hills, their uniform gray streaked with pastel colors in layers of erosion that had exposed the fossilized strata.

Caleb was worried. He had ridden steadily southward attempting to intercept the trail of the Huastecs and his beloved Shanni, but he'd found no trace of the small band. Caleb again reproached himself for allowing them to leave without him, although he'd had no choice. Caleb had been a marked man until Inman's death. Run off his land and almost murdered, Caleb had fought for time and a future as the Huastecs were forced to leave their ancestral home in Mesa Verde. Now he could not find them. The land sprawled in league upon rolling league and his passage left no mark upon it.

Caleb was torn between two worlds. He had risked his life to bring his father's murderers to justice and to reclaim his range. He needed to be at home, rebuilding the range and his future.

But Shanni and Tonah of the Huastecs had saved his life. He had fallen in love with Shanni and wanted her for his wife to share the future he envisioned.

He felt obligated to Tonah, the shaman whose skills had kept him alive, and he respected the old man's wisdom. And yet he felt uncomfortable in Tonah's presence. Tonah was a sorcerer who spoke of projecting his perception into animals to seek information, and of visiting other worlds that influenced events on earth. While Caleb did not doubt that Tonah sincerely believed in the reality of his perceptions, to Caleb they were ill conceived at best, and at worst, insanity.

Caleb's father, John Elias Stone, had been a lay preacher sincere in his belief that the Bible was the Word of God, and interpreted it literally. As a child, Caleb had listened wide-eyed as his father warned his small congregation against the "detestable practices" laid out by Moses in the Old Testament. Caleb remembered that his father's eyes burned intensely as he preached from Deuteronomy against the practice of divination or sorcery, interpreting of omens, engaging in witchcraft or the casting of spells. And now he owed his life to a man he hardly knew who openly believed in and practiced these things.

Shanni, Tonah's granddaughter, had complete confidence in Tonah. She had developed paranormal powers under his tutelage. Now she felt obligated to use her powers to lead the Huastecs on their perilous journey south to the "center" of their civilization, a place that according to their legends had existed hundreds of years ago, and might not exist today.

Caleb had learned to be successful in his world. After meeting Shanni, he had realized that his life would not be complete without Shanni as his wife. But she came from a different world, and somehow they must find a way to bring their two worlds together.

How his life had changed! A year ago he had been riding free in the border country, surviving by his wits and narrowly avoiding the life of an outlaw. Now he had responsibilities and ever-deepening problems to resolve.

As his thoughts returned to the present, the feeling of being watched added to his worry. Caleb's experience in desert country had enabled him to develop a sixth sense for impending danger. He felt that uneasiness now as he scanned the low hills, although he saw nothing that portended danger in the lifeless landscape.

Leading his packhorse, he nudged his mount to the left toward the low range of hills. The horses plodded, heads down with weariness. He would have to stop soon and let the horses rest. They were all in and Caleb knew he could not win a running fight. He continued to scan his surroundings from the shade of his hat brim.

Suddenly his horse shied violently and saved Caleb's life. He heard the soft whirr of the arrow that drove his mount into the air, screaming in agony from the wound in its right lung. Caleb kicked free as the animal fell and scrambled behind the fallen body.

The arrow had come from a small depression to his right. He slipped the carbine from the saddle scabbard and peered intently, blinking back the sweat that ran into his eyes. He turned his head and saw the packhorse standing unhurt. He still had a chance.

He turned his attention back to the depression and caught a slight movement. He laid the carbine across the saddle, tightened his finger on the trigger, and waited. He saw a glimmer of movement and fired. He heard a sharp cry of pain as a dusty body twisted into view. The air sang with arrows as two warriors rushed him. He rolled, firing, as they were upon him. His bullet stopped the first attacker, and he clubbed wildly with the rifle as the second ripped at him savagely with a knife. The man crumpled and stillness returned. Caleb lay, gasping for breath, watching the blood of his attackers soak into the dry sand. He had a flesh wound, but he was alive.

He climbed to his feet and gathered the reins of the packhorse. He walked to the depression and read the tracks of the warriors leading in from the west. The tracks showed the warriors had been following a number of riders on foot and had split off to attack him, likely for his horses. Caleb guessed they were renegades who had lost their horses during a raid. The riders had continued south and that meant trouble for the Huastecs if they were in the area.

Caleb scanned his surroundings. If the riders had turned back, they could be watching him now. He started walking toward cover, every sense alert. He needed water and rest for the horse. He could not evade hostile riders on a tired horse and knew that he would risk death on foot in the desert heat.

Long shadows moved out from the hills as the hours passed and the sun sank slowly in the west. Caleb approached the low hills despite the danger to look for water. He scanned the terrain for any sign of life. Presently he saw slight marks on the sand where the smooth body of a rattlesnake had passed. He followed the path until it disappeared on the hard gravel at the base of the canyon. He turned to walk along the canyon and found dry gullies breaking the wall, evidence of water flow in the past.

He saw that a small pebble had been dislodged, as if overturned by a hoof. The renegades would know the location of any nearby water. Caleb turned a corner and saw the mouth of a small ravine. Likely the riders were ahead of him, but he had to find water.

Time passed slowly as he wound along the twisting ravine, senses alert for danger. The green of a desert plant in the shadow of an overhang caught Caleb's eye and he knew that water was nearby. The ravine widened and he saw where riders had scooped out a depression in the sand and watered in the seep. The seep was damp, the water exhausted for the present, but it would replenish if given time. He settled down to wait.

SHANNI AWAKENED DISTURBED as day was breaking. She looked about confused until the temporary shelter brought her back to reality. She and the Huastecs were somewhere in the desert country on their journey to the Center, their sanctuary far to the south.

She dressed quickly and left the tent to find her grandfather Tonah, shaman of the Huastecs.

She found him away from the temporary camp, sitting quietly in meditation, facing the rising sun.

Tonah perceived her agitation as she approached.

"Good morning, granddaughter. I sense that you did not sleep well."

"My dream-catcher was overwhelmed last night. My sleep was filled with nightmares in which dangerous possibilities churned in chaos, filling me with dread for the days to come."

Tonah silently weighed her words. Each Huastec kept a "dream-catcher", a small hoop of willow with a net of string, near the sleeping area to filter out unpleasant and false dreams while allowing good and truthful ones through. With Shanni's heightened sense of intuition, nightmares that got through her dream-catcher were not to be taken lightly.

"I feel your agitation. As we've discussed previously, Creation is continually churning possibilities for the future, both good and bad. Your dreams may indicate that we're approaching a node of dangerous potential for the Huastecs. We must seek to understand and to proceed with great caution."

"But with your knowledge as a shaman, why can't we foresee the danger and avoid it?" Shanni's voice reflected fatigue combined with concern.

"Because the future is not fixed. Creation itself is not 'solid'. Everything in this world, including you and me, is composed of minute entities, forces that move back and forth between probabilities and essence. When the forces coalesce, they become 'reality' as we know it, and that reality is influenced by what we interpret as good and evil."

"So what I'm perceiving is the potential for evil to befall us."

"Yes. While it is not inevitable, your dreams indicate that we are facing an increased probability of danger."

"What are we to do? We cannot stay here in the desert. We must continue our journey."

"Ask Aurel to bring your dream-catcher and the supplies for the ritual. I will attempt to communicate with the entities caught by your dream-catcher."

Shanni frowned. "But you told me never to attempt that. You said I could become lost in their worlds and be unable to find my way back."

"That is true. Many years of training were required for me to learn to contain my fear and to set the signposts necessary for my return. I would not do this lightly, but to proceed on our journey without understanding this new and powerful threat would be folly."

Shanni nodded with understanding. "I will send Aurel as you wish, and tell our people to wait."

"Ask them to rest but remain vigilant. We do not know how much time we have."

Shanni rose and walked back to the Huastec camp. Already the sun's heat was awakening the hostility of the desert.

Aurel assisted Tonah in stretching a blanket across four poles, creating a canopy in the dry wash where the Huastecs were camped. Tonah carefully fastened Shanni's dream-catcher to a support, adjusting it to hang down between Tonah and the sun.

Tonah sat on a blanket under the canopy, studying the dream-catcher as it swung in a faint breeze. The sun's rays danced along the strands of the web, glistening like dew. Colors flashed as the strands broke the light, prism-like, into ever-changing rainbows of color. The colors began to rotate, forming a vortex that pulled at Tonah, seeking to draw his perception inside. Tonah resisted and reached down to grasp a pebble. He squeezed it tightly in his left hand. It would be his signpost back to the reality of the world of the Huastecs.

The vortex intensified and grew in size, blocking out Tonah's peripheral view. He felt the earth upon which he was sitting start to vibrate as if in an earthquake and knew the sign that his world of "reality" was disintegrating. He felt the primordial fear of his youth, when he had traveled this path for the first time, and held it in rigid control. The body always knew fear. He let the fear flow over him like mist, detached as his energy body floated free and he entered the unlimited worlds of probability. Lurking behind them, he knew, was the unspeakable chaos that pre-existed the creation of the universe.

Tonah exercised his will and stabilized his energy body. He slowed the speed of his spirit body into the vortex and floated in the storm of colors. He knew from past training that he must establish a signpost quickly, an anchor in this "new" world to avoid becoming hopelessly lost with no way to find his way back.

He "spoke" soundlessly. "A Guardian will appear."

He waited. The vortex intensified, attempting to pull him forward. He patiently resisted. The vortex slowed and the dreams caught in the dream-catcher appeared, a phantasmagoria of images, people and events to confuse Tonah as he waited impassively. He was experiencing the nightmares that Shanni had not had to endure. He steeled himself, strengthened by his years of experience.

The images shimmered and a surreal landscape emerged, the shadows and colors oddly juxtaposed, unworldly. A face appeared, and then a body coalesced into a coyote sitting on its haunches looking at Tonah.

"What do you wish?" it "said" silently.

"A signpost to fix these nodal points until I return, and a Guide for my journey."

The coyote raised an eyebrow. "I see you are an experienced traveler. It will be as you wish."

The coyote raised a paw that became a hand, holding a torch that glowed with light but not heat. "This will anchor this 'place' until you return. Where do you wish to 'go'?"

Tonah knew he would go nowhere as he was already nowhere and everywhere in the spirit world. He had to *will* the potential world of danger and he'd simply 'be' there.

"I will be at the node portending danger and I will examine its intent," he said.

The coyote nodded and the surreal world gradually disappeared as the coyote grew, manlike, to sit on a wooden throne. The throne widened to become a screen upon which images moved in the background. Tonah recognized the outline of mountains and valleys, a sere wasteland. Strands like a spider's web extended across and through the images. Light traveled up and down the strands like sliding glass beads.

"Tell me about the potentiality for danger to the Huastecs." Tonah thought, projecting his will.

The image of the coyote dimmed almost into shadow as it spoke. "The journey of the Huastecs is taking place on many levels, some known and some as yet unknown to you. The journey in your primary world is filled with predictable dangers, some of which you must endure to avoid even greater and more life-threatening peril on other levels."

"Do you see Death?"

"There is always death. Nothing exists forever in its present manifestation."

"I mean do you see imminent death for the Huastecs during the journey?"

"The probability is highest if you maintain your present course. While the alternatives you may choose are also dangerous, the probability that most of the Huastecs will survive is increased. No course of action will assure the survival of all your people. That node of possibility is past."

So some of us must die, Tonah thought with sadness. "We must change our present course."

"If you continue on your present course, death is certain for all of your people. The Huastecs will not complete their journey."

The landscape disappeared, leaving only the strands glowing in a world of darkness. The outline of the coyote began to fade.

"Wait," Tonah said forcefully. "I would have another signpost." Tonah willed the image of the coyote to stop and it stabilized.

"I cannot help you further. I must go now."

"A signpost. I will not release you without a signpost."

"You are strong. As you will."

A star-like object began to glow faintly in the blackness, a blue-white radiance almost absorbed by the overwhelming darkness. Tonah felt waves of dread wash over him and knew he was entering the worst of Shanni's nightmares at a level even she would not remember.

"I would have a Guide," he said. He steeled himself and waited.

A barely-perceptual human-like image outlined in a black shroud began to emerge from the darkness.

"You summoned me, and you awaken me at your peril."

"You initiated the contact by injecting yourself into my world. I would know why."

"I do not wish to answer."

"In this world you are compelled to answer. That is why I came. I will you to answer."

"Very well. There are forces being awakened by the journey of the Huastecs. You seek sanctuary, but your movement is upsetting the matrix of the Center. There is the potential to affect ancient power relationships long dormant. As you threaten the power of others, they recognize the danger and will resist."

"How will I know them?"

"That is of your world, not mine. I do not have to answer."

The image transfigured, and Tonah saw the image of an old man, sitting before a fire, his face lost in shadow. The reek of death and decay swept over Tonah and he set himself against the perception of evil. He heard the man laugh softly to himself, then reach out to douse the fire.

The sudden darkness engulfed Tonah, threatening to disorient him. He steadied himself and stared, concentrating on the star-like signpost. The glow of the signpost emerged slowly from the darkness and he used it as a springboard back to the world of the coyote. The coyote was gone.

Tonah felt his strength waning and knew he must hasten the return to his world. He lifted his left hand and stared at the pebble he still gripped tightly. The surreal world shattered into fragments of light, and nausea swept through him as the universe trembled and the strands of the dream-catcher suddenly popped into view. He released the pebble and wiped the perspiration from his brow.

He trembled, as from a chill. Aurel leapt to his feet, threw a blanket around Tonah's shoulders, and held a canteen for Tonah to drink.

Chapter 2

Hot wind off the desert stirred Shanni's hair as she gazed into the distance. Arid hills rolled away in all directions, giving no relief to the eye and no help in finding a path through the wilderness. She turned to Matal and read the concern in his eyes. Matal was barely out of his teens, but his natural ability and good humor had already made him an informal leader of the Huastec warriors. He too was overwhelmed by the vastness of this land. Nothing in the experience of the Huastecs had prepared them for the journey and her gift of prescience could only provide limited assistance.

Shanni was uneasy. All day she had felt that evil was stalking her people. She turned to look at the small canyon where the Huastecs were resting from the day's trek. She knew they must find assistance soon. Privation had overcome them during the past weeks. Game was scarce and the search for water was a never-ending battle. Even Tonah, who had served so well as the spiritual leader of the Huastecs, had come to realize the enormity of their undertaking. Again she felt the burden upon her as the others trusted her gifts for guidance.

"Come, Matal, we must return to the others," Shanni said, careful to mask the uncertainty in her voice. She led down the gravelly slope.

"What did you see?" He questioned. "Is there better land to the south?"

"We only saw more of the same, endless."

"The people are weary and must find rest. We must find sanctuary."

"Yes," Shanni agreed. She paced, unable to decide what to do. She turned and climbed back up the promontory. A glimmer of movement caught her eye and she peered carefully, pointing it out to Matal.

"I see it," he said. "There are half a dozen or more riders on our back trail."

His voice was steady. Shanni was struck by how quickly Matal was growing from a boy into a man. The hardships of the journey had matured the young people. They were fighting for the survival of the Huastecs.

She returned her gaze to the distance and began to make out the dim riders, hours away but moving purposefully. Should they wait and hope for aid or would they be risking attack? Did the strange riders cause her feeling of dread? She could not tell and felt helpless in this wilderness.

She returned to Tonah, who read her agitation. "There are strangers on our back trail, many hours back."

Tonah motioned Shanni and the young warriors to gather around him.

"I walked in the spirit world to examine Shanni's dreams. I was warned that without help we would all perish. The alternative is to seek the aid of strangers, which is also dangerous. We will suffer but the probability is that most of us will survive. We must decide."

Matal spoke firmly, "We have no alternative but to seek their help. However, we must minimize the risk. I suggest we select a group to reveal to the riders when they catch up to us. I and one other will wait for them and seek their help."

The others nodded their assent.

"I will join you," Tonah agreed, "For I will need to perceive their spirit."

"Perhaps I should stay also," Shanni offered.

"We cannot risk it," Tonah answered. "If they attack us, you and Aurel must lead the others to safety."

He's right, Shanni thought, as a shiver ran through her. If only Caleb were here. He knew how to deal with this harsh world on its own terms. He would know what to do. The Huastecs warriors were courageous, but there had been little time to train them in the use of the rifles. They would be no match for seasoned fighters.

At Matal's direction, the Huastecs hurried to break camp. As the group moved farther up the canyon, young men followed behind brushing away the signs of their passage in the gravel. Soon the main body of the Huastecs was hidden and Matal and Tonah climbed the promontory and settled down to wait.

The strangers traveled swiftly and entered the canyon where Tonah and Matal waited by mid-afternoon. Two of the riders were out front, their gazes intent on the canyon floor tracking the Huastecs. Five other riders followed closely. They were lean men, dusty warriors of a tribe unknown to Tonah. These men were hunters, he thought. They knew how to kill, but were they hunters of men?

Tonah sat with only part of his body visible to the oncoming riders, yet one of the sharp-eyed pursuers saw him from afar and halted abruptly. The other riders caught up to him and they spoke briefly. The men fanned out across the trail with rifles ready and urged their horses forward at a walk. As they neared, a tall rider, evidently the leader, hailed Tonah in a language he did not understand.

He answered in Spanish. "I am Tonah of the Huastecs. I come in peace, seeking aid. Who are you and will you help us?"

The man considered Tonah's words as his men scanned the surroundings. He answered in broken Spanish, "I am Kaibito of the Navaho. I do not know the Huastec tribe. How do you come to be in Navaho lands?"

"We came from the north, the land of big mountains with white peaks. We journey to our homeland to the south, but we are lost and need your guidance to food and water. We will then leave your lands and continue our journey."

"Where is the remainder of your people?"

"They are hidden until we determine that you come in peace and mean us no harm."

"Very well. We will help you. Do you have weapons?"

"Yes."

"Throw them out to us. You will not need them."

"The Huastecs come in peace, but we are not fools. We do not ask for your weapons, and we will keep ours."

Tonah saw anger flare in Kaibito's eyes and felt the man's distrust. He and Matal must remain vigilant.

Kaibito covered quickly, " As you wish, but we must hurry. We have far to go to reach water before nightfall."

Matal rode up the canyon and selected a small group of Huastecs, mostly young warriors and old men. The main band of Huastecs, containing the women and children, would remain hidden, near the water hole, until Matal and the others could return for them. They could not risk revealing the presence of the main band to Kaibito and his riders.

Matal and the small group of Huastec men returned down the canyon and Kaibito led away to the west.

The hours dragged in the heat and the dust and Kaibito was impatient with the slow progress of the Huastecs. The horses plodded steadily, their bodies lathered from the heat.

They continued traveling as dusk fell, entering rough terrain with impassable rock slides. Walls of sheer rock, extending upward hundreds of feet, replaced the weathered hills. The towering mesas reminded Tonah of Mesa Verde. How he would have liked to finish his days in peace in those wild but familiar mesas that had been home to his people.

The riders pushed on without rest, driven by the promise of water at Kaibito's destination. The riders turned to enter a narrow canyon that branched out into a natural park. Tonah noted the fresh breeze that soughed down from the heights. The riders dismounted and led the horses on foot. In an overhang of the cliff there was a series of natural tanks containing water. The tired travelers moved forward to quench their thirst.

Kaibito's riders were well provisioned to be travelers, Tonah thought, and was grateful when Kaibito shared generously with the Huastecs. Fires were built and food prepared as the tired Huastecs settled down for the night. Kaibito moved about with intensity, his dark eyes taking in everything as he gave orders and posted riders out to guard the camp. More than once Shanni felt his stare, but she ignored him and moved away from the firelight to mind the children and become less conspicuous to the men. After eating, the exhausted Huastecs began bedding down, sleeping as a group away from Kaibito and his riders. Matal posted Huastec guards outside camp away from Kaibito's men as a precaution.

At daybreak, Tonah awakened and stood up, scanning his surroundings. He stretched and walked out to view the park, an oasis of green hidden away in the gray canyons. He saw that the runoff of water from the tanks supported a coarse grass in the park, providing graze for the horses. The Huastecs were rekindling the fires and preparing breakfast. Kaibito had led them to a place where they could rest and renew their strength.

The sentries were not in sight as Tonah strode to Kaibito's camp.

"Please join us, Tonah," Kaibito welcomed. "We have fresh coffee."

Kaibito stood up, smiling, and Tonah saw the Huastec sentries sitting near the fire. They looked at him bleakly and the realization struck Tonah that they were Kaibito's prisoners.

Chapter 3

Kaibito's black eyes flashed as he surveyed the camp. His men carried out their chores, avoiding his glance. More than one of his riders had felt his wrath.

Kaibito's mind was busy with his plans. They could not tarry in this place. They must move, and quickly, to the refuge from pursuing soldiers that he had built to the west. Kaibito hated the white-eyes with unremitting passion and his raids were the terror of the frontier. His people, under the leadership of Manuelito, had come to terms with the military leaders of the whites and settled on reservations, but Kaibito had remained unconquered. He had contemptuously broken with Manuelito, leading his renegades in a guerrilla war that would end only with his death.

The latest raid had not gone well. Kaibito had lost men and horses, and a few of his fighters had been forced to flee on foot. It had been an omen of changing fortune to stumble upon a lone white rider with two horses. He had left the horseless men to take the horses and catch up while he and the remaining riders tracked the Huastecs.

The colony he was establishing at his refuge needed workers. Kaibito intended to make the Huastecs his slaves, providing sustenance for his base while freeing his men to continue the raids. He was growing impatient. His men should have taken the horses and caught up by now. They would feel his wrath for delaying his travel!

Kaibito called to his lieutenant, Chama, who hurried over. "The men we left to obtain the white rider's horses have not caught up. Send someone to find them and direct them to us, for we cannot wait."

"It will be done right away," Chama replied and moved away to address the men busy loading the horses. A tall, lithe rider disengaged from the group and rode away to the east.

Kaibito returned to the campfire where Tonah and the two Huastec sentries waited.

"Kaibito would speak with you," he said, motioning Tonah to step away from the others. "You are our prisoners. You will do as I direct. Any resistance and the men will be killed. You are to see that my orders are obeyed without question."

Tonah started to protest, but Kaibito struck him across the face. "Do not question me. Your people live at my whim."

Kaibito's eyes smoldered. "Prepare your people to move out quickly."

Tonah returned to the Huestecs' camp. Shanni had witnessed Kaibito's assault and moved to see if Tonah was hurt.

"I've been our undoing," he said, his voice shaking. "I have delivered us into the hands of a brutal enemy."

Matal turned and shook his head, "Do not blame yourself. We have food and water and we are alive. As your dream predicted, this is the lesser of two evils. We will find a way to overcome Kaibito and his men when the time comes."

"Kaibito has threatened to kill us if we do not do his bidding," Tonah responded. "We must go along with him for now."

Matal gave the order to break camp, "Make haste to travel. We must not anger Kaibito."

Shanni saw the rebellion in Matal's eyes as he turned away. He and the other men would fight and risk death to escape their captors, but they must not give their lives in vain. Their hope was to stay alive, learn the ways of this harsh land, and wait for a favorable time to attack. Even if they were to escape now, they would be at the mercy of the desert. She and Tonah must keep the young men under control.

They moved out in the heat of the day, traveling westward. Kaibito was restless and occasionally his men would return to threaten Huastec stragglers. The travel was hardest on the children and old people, but the young men assisted and they continued moving.

Toward evening Shanni noticed that they were climbing into higher elevations as the landscape changed into great canyons and mesas.

She spoke to Matal: "Be sure to note our back trail. All these canyons look alike, and we will have to find our way back when we escape."

Matal nodded, "I've been memorizing landmarks, but with no trail to return to, we may be as well off to select our direction and proceed."

Shanni thought a moment. They were indeed lost whether or not they were with Kaibito's band. Their journey was based on the faith that they could reach their homeland. It was a slender thread, but it was all they had.

· The desert cooled as the sun set, casting long shadows from the canyon walls The route led along a rocky valley enclosed by sheer rock walls. At a turn, they entered a natural park nestled bowl-like in the rocky prominences. Shanni saw the foundations of ancient stone buildings, now gray with dust, extending outward in geometric patterns. She overheard one of Kaibito's men refer to the valley in Spanish as the "canon de Chaco", Chaco Canyon. Like Mesa Verde, people had once lived here and now they were gone, she thought. She felt a pang as the ruins reminded her of the Anasazi city she had visited with Caleb. Were all the Ancients long dead and forgotten? Was the Huastecs' quest to return to their people futile? She fought the despair that welled up inside her.

As they approached the far side of the valley, Shanni saw a prominence appear in the vast face of the sheer wall. In the lengthening shadows, she recognized ancient dwellings in the face of the cliff. Others, like the Huastecs, had once made their homes in the protection of the cliffs, but there was no welcome glow of cooking fires. The crumbling stone faced blankly into the timeless canyon. They passed the cliff and entered another narrow canyon.

Tonah paused and sniffed the air. "There is water ahead."

Matal, riding slightly ahead of Tonah and Shanni, turned. "Yes, I detected it also, and it is more than a seep to be carried this far upon the air. We must be nearing their base."

The horses quickened their pace and the canyon widened into a small glade. Grass covered the gravelly ground and small plants clung to the weathered walls of the canyon. Natural basins held water in an overhang of rock and nearby were the dwellings of Kaibito's people.

"It is not a large group," Matal observed. "Hardly more than a dozen women and children. We are nearly as many. How long can they support us here?"

As the Huastecs gathered gratefully to quench their thirst, Shanni studied the women and children who stood looking at them. The women stared balefully. Shanni shuddered; they were not welcome here.

Kaibito moved among the Huastecs, shouting orders. He presented a fearful visage as he turned, rifle in hand with a wicked knife belted around his waist.

"You!" He pointed at Shanni. "You will go to my lodge." His eyes burned into hers a moment and then he turned away.

Shanni trembled as she moved to comply.

A fat, squat women stepped out of the shadows as she approached the door of the crude dwelling and Shanni felt a wave of hate as the woman glared at her. The woman pointed to a pot of food simmering over the campfire. Shanni ate hurriedly. The woman reappeared and motioned her to enter the doorway. As Shanni entered, she was led to a small side room with a pallet on the dirt floor. The woman shoved Shanni toward the pallet and left the room.

Shanni huddled in the corner, pulling the rough blanket about her. She shuddered and closed her eyes to shut out her surroundings as exhaustion claimed her and she fell asleep.

Chapter 4

Kaibito and Chama stood on a rise overlooking the camp as the Huastec men were herded along the canyon wall. They would work the silver mine, helping Kaibito to finance his dream of unremitting war upon the white invaders. Kaibito had fought alongside Manuelito and had accompanied the Navahos on the "long walk" to Bosque Redondo. There he had watched his people die of malnutrition and of the epidemics that came from the hated whites. He had escaped and vowed to visit a war of unprecedented proportions upon all whites until the Navaho lands were returned and forever secure. He had learned many things during his enforced stay on the reservation. The superior technology of the whites offset the fighting ability of his warriors. He had studied the white soldiers' weapons and learned the value of silver in purchasing the tools of war.

He turned to Chama. "Now we have the means to buy the rifles we need. Push these slaves hard. We need the silver quickly. Even now, the men with the guns should be arriving in Mexico to meet with us. There is no time to lose."

Chama nodded. "The Huastecs are untrained and appear weak. Likely many will die before they become productive."

"So be it. We cannot wait."

Chama nodded again. He understood the importance of the silver, but he did not want to risk Kaibito's wrath. Slaves were difficult to find and bring to the camp. He did not want to be blamed if the Huastecs died.

The Huastec men were pushed into a dimly lit mine shaft and set to work under the scrutiny of one of Chama's men. They dug with pickaxes and shovels, and Matal noted with alarm that there was no shoring up of the tunnel. A rockslide could bury them at any moment.

He called out to the guard. "We need to shore up this tunnel! We need wood to make supports."

The guard stared at him without response.

"We cannot get the silver out if the tunnel collapses. We must shore up the mine shaft." Matal realized that the guard did not understand him, but apparently picked up the urgency in his voice.

The guard called to another man further down the canyon. The man mounted a horse and rode away toward camp. Presently he returned accompanied by the man Matal recognized as Chama.

Chama spoke in Spanish, evidently not pleased. "The guard says you are talking instead of working. If it happens again, you will be punished."

"I told the guard that the tunnel is unsafe. We must have wood to shore it up or it will collapse."

Chama smiled evilly, "And where do you think we would find wood? Look around, do you see a forest?"

"We must find a way to shore up the tunnel."

"There is no time for that."

"Even if you do not value our lives, you cannot get the silver out if the tunnel collapses."

"That's a risk we will have to take. Now get back to work and I'd better not be interrupted again."

Without waiting for a reply, Chama turned and rode to the guard. After a brief conversation, he turned and rode back toward the camp.

Aurel was working nearby and had overheard Matal's appeal. "It is clear that we are expendable. They want only the silver."

"Yes," Matal replied. "And quickly. After they have the silver, they will not need us and will kill us. We have only a little time to find a way to escape."

"We cannot escape on foot. Kaibito's men would ride us down."

"Then we must find a way to kill Kaibito and his men!"

Aurel remained silent, stunned. Their cause was hopeless if that was their alternative. They had to find another way.

Shanni was awakened rudely by the woman and ordered to begin the day's chores. She ground maize into meal, tended the cook fire, and performed other duties pointed out by the woman's gestures and grunts. When Shanni was too slow, the woman enforced her wishes with shouts and shoves. Only the curious stares of the children broke the distress of her first day as the servant of the woman addressed as Hosta.

Tonah and the older adults had been assigned to tend the small plots of vegetables growing along the dry wash. As Shanni watched out of the corners of her eyes, she saw Tonah carrying water from the basin and was reminded of the Huastecs' fields in Mesa Verde. It seemed so long ago. Could it be only a few weeks since they left on their journey south? How long could they remain here without hope of escape or rescue?

What had happened to Caleb? Had the desert claimed him too? Despair overcame Shanni as she closed off her thoughts and applied herself to the tasks.

She was watching when the Huastec men returned to camp for the night. She moved over to join them at the campfire, eating her food beside Tonah.

"I perceive that the danger increases the longer we stay here."

Tonah nodded. "The dream walking only indicated this was a better alternative, not that it was a good one. Still I have faith that we will not perish here."

"We cannot escape, and they will not keep us after our usefulness is over. Do you think they will release us?"

"We must keep up hope. In the meantime, we must look for alternatives to develop. We must continue our dream walking to find a way."

"It is very difficult when we are distracted by the danger around us."

"Yes, but that is when it is most necessary."

The woman Hosta shouted across the camp and motioned for Shanni to come to the dwelling. Dread welled up in Shanni. She had hoped she'd be allowed to stay with her people for the night. So far Kaibito had been busy and ignored her, but she knew the implications of his interest. She would rather die than submit to him, but if she resisted he might take it out on the other Huastecs. She purposely did not clean up before retiring, preferring discomfort rather than to appear desirable. She could hear Hosta padding about outside as she lay down on her pallet. She thought she heard a male voice but Kaibito did not appear. She remembered Tonah's admonition, and attempted to calm herself to spirit walk, but she was too tired and distressed. Soon she gave up and fell asleep.

Hosta awakened her early the next morning and Shanni was already at work at her chores when Kaibito's men appeared from the canyon with loaded pack mules. They saddled horses in preparation for a journey. Kaibito strode among the men, giving commands and checking the packs. When the loading was completed, he returned to the dwelling. He stopped to address Hosta. Shanni could not understand the words but she understood Hosta's whining protest as she turned and disappeared into the shadowy doorway.

Kaibito turned to Shanni. "I have spoken to Hosta," he said in Spanish. "You will not be mistreated while I am away. When I return, you will be my woman."

Kaibito turned and walked to his horse. Shanni's senses were reeling as he mounted and led the caravan down the valley.

Chapter 5

The morning sun awakened Caleb and he rose, stretching out the stiffness in his limbs. He saw that water had accumulated in the seep during the night. He quenched his thirst, filled the canteen, and then untied the horse to allow it to drink. He mounted and rode up the cut in the bank onto a ridge where he could survey the country. Weathered hills cut by gullies and canyons met his gaze. He sat pondering whether to continue south in search of the Huastecs. Finally he decided to follow the riders from the previous day. There were no trails and they had shown they knew where to find water. He would turn south when he found a stream to follow. The riders had not attempted to hide their trail. The tracks showed they had been pushing their horses, unwise in this desert unless one had a near destination in mind. Maybe there was an Indian camp ahead and where there was a camp, there would be water.

Hours passed as he continued westward. In the sandy bed of a canyon he saw where the riders had cut the trail of a larger group and he saw the telltale tracks of travois. Was the band he was following part of a larger band? Or had they somehow overtaken the Huastecs? He increased his caution. The warriors he left lifeless on the sand had shown the group would be hostile.

His trained eyes the tracks as he walked the horse slowly up the canyon. The riders had changed position, moving from single file to ride four abreast. That was a defensive position for a running fight. They expected trouble.

Caleb dismounted to work out the message of the tracks. Two men on foot had met the riders as they continued up the canyon, and then abruptly the tracks vanished. Caleb circled without success to pick up the trail. The men had deliberately hidden their trail at this point when they had not bothered to do so before. Why? He gathered his horse's reins and started to remount when a bullet knocked him off his feet. The sound of a rifle an instant later echoed off the walls of the canyon.

Caleb's ears buzzed and he could not clear his vision. His pulse hammered in his temples as he rolled into a depression and lay still, trying to clear his senses. He pulled his revolver free of the holster and waited. The slight scuff of moccasins warned him to roll over and he fired without aiming. The attacker fell heavily and clawed in the dirt to crawl away. Caleb tried to raise his head to see but a great weariness came over him. He lay back in the sun and lost consciousness.

Caleb felt a warm tongue lick his face and heard a whine. He opened his eyes to starlight and saw the dog that stood over him in the cool twilight. He turned his head. An Indian boy squatted on his heels, studying him. When Caleb tried to speak, the boy jumped up and bounded away, followed by the dog. Caleb wondered if he was hallucinating. There was a metallic taste in his mouth and he was thirsty. He must move and get to shelter. The boy returned with an old man. The man lifted a canteen to Caleb's lips and he drank. The Indian spoke but Caleb did not know the language. He tried a reply in Spanish and the man's eyes lit in recognition.

"Lie still. Tsiping will help you," the man responded in Spanish.

Tsiping moved out of sight and minutes later Caleb heard the steps of a horse approaching. The old man and the boy helped Caleb climb on the crude travois the man had constructed. As they moved away the motion sent pain racing through Caleb's body and he cried out.

"I am sorry for the pain, but it is only a little way," Tsiping said. "We must get you to camp where we can help you."

When Caleb regained consciousness, his wound had been dressed and he was bundled comfortably near a campfire. He heard bleating and turned his head to see Tsiping and the boy keeping watch over the sheep grazing nearby.

Tsiping saw that Caleb had awakened and walked over. "The wound is not serious but you lost a lot of blood. You will be sore and weak for a few days. Here, I have some broth for you."

Caleb managed a few sips and looked around. "Where am I, and what tribe do you belong to?"

"We are a day's ride from Manuelito's camp. He is chief of the Navaho. I will take you to Manuelito and he will decided how best to help you." Caleb started to rise but pain coursed through him and he lay back. He was in no condition to fend for himself.

"Very well."

"Good. Sleep now. We go as soon as you can travel."

The camp was large and located in a bend of the Chaco River. Tsiping led Caleb past curious onlookers to a dwelling set back from the bank of the river.

"That's Manuelito," Tsiping said as a tall man emerged from the teepee and watched them approach. Tsiping addressed Manuelito briefly and Caleb recognized the word "espanol". Apparently Tsiping was advising that Caleb understood Spanish.

Manuelito, stately in leather trimmed with silver and turquoise, addressed Caleb in perfect Spanish.

"Welcome to our camp. Please come in and tell me how we may help you."

Caleb followed into the teepee and explained the events that had brought him here. When Caleb finished, Manuelito considered for a few moments before he spoke.

"Manuelito has put war behind him. We Navaho only want to live without further violence. You are on the Navaho reservation, given back to us after the Nahondzod, the Fearing Time, when we were moved by the pony soldiers to the Pecos. There our people perished and I journeyed to the white leader to petition for our people's return to our land. While our wish was finally granted, not all of us could see the wisdom of submission. One of our greatest warriors, Kaibito, broke with us and continues to make war. I believe it was his men who attacked you. I hear of his raids and fear that he will bring grief to all our people."

"Can't you tell the soldiers where he is?"

"We do not know the location of Kaibito's camp. He has warned us not to try to find him or he would retaliate against us. Manuelito walks a narrow path to protect his people. I want no more trouble with the soldiers."

Caleb related the meeting of two men with Kaibito's riders in the canyon.

"I do not believe that the men were Navaho. We have only lone sheepherders and their families in the outlying areas."

James Gibson

Caleb weighed the information. Could Kaibito have stumbled upon the Huastecs? And if so where was the remainder of the group? He felt dread come over him. Had Shanni become a prisoner of the renegades? He'd have to trust Manuelito in order to secure his help.

"There is a large group known as the Huastecs traveling south. I'm trying to find them to help in their journey back to their homeland. I'm concerned that they might have been captured by Kaibito and his men."

"Kaibito was once a great warrior and I relied on his wisdom, but now his hatred for the whites has filled his mind with sickness. Rumor is that he is building an army in the wilds and using slaves to carry out necessary work to support their living. If your Huastecs have fallen in with Kaibito, I fear for them. He may kill them when he is through with them, or they may perish if the pony soldiers hunt him down."

Caleb read the concern in Manuelito's voice, and he understood Manuelito's quandary. Manuelito was trying to be helpful while surviving enemies on both sides. A commotion outside brought Manuelito to his feet and Caleb followed him outside. A rider had come in to inform him that soldiers were approaching the camp.

"It is as I feared," Manuelito said. "Kaibito will bring calamity upon us all."

Chapter 6

Lieutenant Porter was a heavy-set man, gruff and pragmatic. As he saw it, his job was to hunt Indians and he pursued it with a single-minded purpose. He wasted no time fretting about the reasons or the necessity for what he did. He had his orders and he kept pushing forward.

He and his men had bivouacked overnight near Manuelito's camp. After rest and a good breakfast, Porter was ready to get down to business and he felt that he knew how to "talk turkey" to an Indian.

Manuelito and Caleb rose to welcome Porter as he approached. "Welcome to Manuelito's lodge. This is Caleb Stone, who is our guest. Would you share our food?"

"No, thanks, Chief. I've eaten, but I've come for some serious talk." Porter spit a stream of tobacco juice.

"What is it you wish?" Manuelito answered, motioning to a seat in the shade.

"First, I need to understand who you are and why you're here," Porter turned to Caleb. "No offense, but I'm on official business."

"None taken," Caleb replied. Porter would be foolish to discuss business in front of a stranger. Caleb summarized his attempt to overtake the Huastecs and his run-in with hostiles.

Porter seemed satisfied with Caleb's explanation and turned back to Manuelito. "There was a raid over east a few days ago. A settler and some field hands were killed. We've been sent to find the guilty parties and take them back to Fort Wingate. The trail headed west so we figure they're Navaho. We want you to turn them over to us."

Porter wasn't one to mince words, Caleb thought as Manuelito considered quietly before answering.

"None of my warriors have left the reservation. You have Manuelito's word. If they are Navaho, they are not of my group and we know nothing of such a raid."

Porter grunted and turned to Caleb. "What do you know about this?"

"I was riding south when I was ambushed by a small band traveling west. They could have been the raiders. The ones who attacked me were on foot and I think they were after my horses. For what it's worth, I believe Manuelito."

"Ahuh. Well, I figure if he warn't in on it, he knows who was. How about it, Chief?"

"I do not know of the raiders. You know that my former war chief, Kaibito, broke with me when we returned to the reservation. He rode away with some men to the wild country to the west. We do not know where he is or what he does."

"Kaibito, huh? Well, I'd guessed he'd be tied up in this. Reckon you'll just have to help us find him."

"That I cannot do," Manuelito answered. "Kaibito swore retribution if we interfered with him. We have laid down our weapons and submitted to the white man. We would be defenseless against Kaibito."

"Look, I ain't got all day. It's dry along the Pecos this time of year. I'd hate to see you go back because you wouldn't cooperate with the U.S. government."

Manuelito's eyes flashed and he looked away. Caleb saw that Manuelito had no choice. No matter what the price, his people could not return to the feared Bosque Redondo.

"I will give you two of my best trackers to ride as scouts. They will help you all they can. I'll see to it. I can do no more for you."

Porter weighed the offer. It would be unwieldy to take more and he figured that Manuelito knew better than to lead him on a wild-goose chase. Likely it was the best he could get.

"Done, and I'm anxious to leave. Round them up and send 'em down pronto."

Porter turned to Caleb, "What about you?"

"Reckon I'll ride along. I can't stay here and I've nearly been killed riding alone. I'll accompany you until I strike the trail of the Huastecs."

"Come along, then. I want to get moving."

Porter hurried away as Caleb turned to thank Manuelito for his hospitality.

"Be careful with Lieutenant Porter," Manuelito said. "He does not weigh his actions. Be careful that you do not come to further grief riding with him!"

Caleb nodded his understanding. It was good advice. Caleb saw the tragedy of Manuelito and the Navaho. He'd caught the fire in Manuelito's eyes at Porter's threat. Manuelito had to be circumspect and balance the opposing forces in an attempt to assure the survival of his people. The Indian wars were still being fought on the plains and soldiers were measured on results. Manuelito was buying time the only way he could. He might have to sacrifice Kaibito for the greater good of the Navaho.

Caleb joined Porter's troop and they rode out from the Navaho camp. The first day's travel took them along the Chaco River westward into increasingly rugged country. The horses were fresh from their rest at camp and made good time. They saw an occasional sheepherder tending his flock, but intercepted no sign of riders on the move.

"Way I figure it," Porter said to Caleb the second day out from Manuelito's camp, "Kaibito's got to have water same as any man. With a sizable group of men and horses, I reckon he'll hang near a river or such. We'll find him and take him back dead or alive. I don't care much which."

Caleb started to answer and thought better of it. No point in alienating Porter. He might need his help if they stumbled upon the Huastecs.

Porter read Caleb's silence as disapproval.

"Reckon you think I'm harsh, but I saw the flies on the bodies of those settlers. We're here to protect them in a country so big it takes weeks to ride across it. The only way is to hunt down and kill every renegade and that's what I aim to do. The people in Washington recently replaced General Carlson out here, so I reckon that's a signal of what the powers that be want us to do."

He's right, Caleb thought. The Indian wars still raged and scandal after scandal rocked the new Indian Bureau. The country was binding up its wounds from the Civil War and had neither stomach nor funding for the Indian problem.

Carlson had tried to be humane and he had been replaced. Hound them into submission or kill them was the prevailing attitude. Let the soldiers handle it, and don't ask questions.

The Huastecs and Shanni were out there somewhere trying to survive these turbulent times. He had to find them and lead them to safety before they got caught up in the Indian wars.

One of Manuelito's scouts returned. "We found sign of riders passing, but they were heading south."

"How many?" Porter asked.

"Maybe a dozen. They were keeping to hard ground. Very difficult to track."

"Let's have a look." Porter waved the troop forward following the scout up the gullied canyon.

Caleb could barely discern the hoof marks pointed out by the scout. Manuelito had kept his word. These were able men.

Caleb moved closer to listen as Porter conferred with his men. Sergeant Carter, a grizzled veteran whose florid face spoke of his lifelong devotion to strong drink, was having his say.

"The trail's cold. They passed through days ago. Best we could do is back trail them and try to find their camp. Like as not, they're on another raid and will be returning."

Porter disagreed. "Better to trail them and ambush them on the way back. We might lose days trying to find their camp."

"That's true," Carter replied, "but they might not come back the same way. In fact, it's likely they won't. The renegades know these wilds, and lots of alternate trails. They'll be hard to catch, but cut off their water and supplies and they'll have to come to ground. 'Sides, if we lose their back trail we're no worse off. We'd have to come back here and try to trail 'em"

"Makes sense." Porter nodded, and gave the order for the troop to fan out, scanning the scant impressions of the riders' passage.

The heat of the day coated men and horses with sweat. A fine dust settled blending the riders into a uniform gray as they moved forward. The hours dragged, becoming an endurance test for man and horse.

In the afternoon they entered rougher country as the low, sandy hills were replaced with high-walled canyons of solid granite, their long shadows providing respite from the blazing sun.

Caleb was dozing in the saddle when he felt a presence, a dread that snapped him awake. It was like a dream, but he was awake. The landscape shimmered and he felt light-headed. Fear struck and he felt himself recoil. The landscape settled and he wiped perspiration from his brow with a bandanna.

A rifle shot echoed off the canyon walls as one of the scouts doubled over his saddle and slid to the ground. Men and horses plunged in the narrow canyon as Porter shouted the men back.

Caleb and Carter spurred ahead, turning a corner to find the bottleneck widened into a park of gravelly washes and broken rock. A bullet caught Carter and he crumpled, falling limply from his racing horse. Caleb gained the shelter of a rock outcropping and returned fire at the attackers. He fired carefully, conserving his ammunition. He didn't like being cut off from the troop, and the fight, judging by the sound, was being carried back down the canyon.

He looked around to find a way out. A low wash wound out of sight nearby. He crawled swiftly and rolled into the sandy bottom. With luck, he could reach the broken gullies that led out of the park. He reached the first corner as bullets spread dust and gravel.

He turned to peer toward the sounds of the rifles when a heavy voice broke the stillness.

"Drop your weapon or you die now!"

Caleb pitched his rifle away and climbed to his feet. He recognized the man who had attacked him near the sheepherder's camp. The man grinned evilly as he turned to another rider.

"This is the one who killed our friends. Kaibito will be pleased that we saved this one for him!"

Chapter 7

Tonah awakened at dawn while the others remained sleeping. He lay still, regulating his breathing, and drew his awareness into himself, concentrating and focusing his energy. He gathered his strength and reached out, projecting his awareness into the world between the worlds, to the "place" where all things were possible but not yet manifest.

His focus narrowed, sensing, and he found himself in a strange place. He felt the stone beneath him and realized he was on a mountain gazing over a vast wasteland. He looked down at furry paws that rested on the ledge, the paws of a small rodent. Through its eyes he saw the soldiers riding far below. He felt a disturbance in the nether world, like a pressure wave that swept across him and then narrowed into a beam of unseen energy that focused on one of the dust-covered riders. Tonah felt the energy attack, but the rider was mentally strong and instinctively resisted.

Tonah launched his awareness at the energy, riding along the beam like a child sliding down a hill. The beam that was awareness recognized Tonah's probe and disengaged, recoiling to its source, trying to leave Tonah behind.

He clung to the receding vortex doggedly, following until he found his awareness in a ground squirrel hidden among the rocks watching a campfire. Seated nearby was an old Indian, eyes half-closed, staring into the fire. The last remnants of the vortex swirled around the man in multi-colored sparks and disappeared.

The man stirred, as if from a dream, and awakened as his awareness returned. He was the source of the beam of energy, Tonah realized. No one would guess that power came from a man of such common appearance.

But why had he chosen to project the power onto a group of soldiers? Tonah knew the expenditure of energy necessary to generate the power. One did not waste one's strength foolishly. There had to be a strong motivation.

He searched his memory, recalling what he had seen and examining every detail. Sorting through each dust-covered rider, he realized the rider the power had attacked was not one of the soldiers, but a civilian riding with them, a man he recognized as Caleb Stone.

Tonah returned his awareness to the ground squirrel and watched as the man got up slowly and seized a stick from the fire. The man turned, his eyes blazing, and hurled the firebrand at the hidden squirrel.

An evil laugh rang in Tonah's ears as he disengaged his awareness and flashed back to the dawn at Kaibito's camp.

Shanni used Kaibito's parting words as a wedge to force Hosta and Chama to give her the run of the camp. She desperately needed to come up with some plan for the escape of the Huastecs before Kaibito returned. Her prescience told her their danger increased with each day.

Matal and the other men were kept near the mines, out of reach. Only Tonah was nearby, but surrounded by guards.

She approached Chama eating his breakfast at the campfire.

"I wish to visit the ruins, and want Tonah to go with me."

"No. All of you are to remain here until Kaibito gets back."

"Kaibito told me he had spoken to you and Hosta. I am not to be treated like a prisoner."

"Go about camp as you wish, but it is too dangerous for you at the ruins."

"What danger can there be out in the open? Are you afraid I'll outrun your riders on foot?"

Chama glared at her and Shanni tried another tack.

"I only want to see the ruins and I feel safe with Tonah. If Kaibito were here, he would allow me to go. Do I have to tell him of your treatment while he was gone?"

Chama thought a moment. She just might try to create an issue with Kaibito. What harm could they do at the ruins, anyway?

"Very well, but I'm sending a guard along to watch you."

"That's fine. We'll only be gone a little while."

She and Tonah walked down the canyon with their guard riding a few steps behind. They conversed in the Huastec language knowing the guard would not understand.

"We must develop a plan of escape, and soon," Shanni said, "I fear it will be too late when Kaibito returns."

"I agree," Tonah replied, "But we must plan for stealth and subterfuge. We cannot hope to outrun them. Our quandary is where to hide after we escape. We cannot move fast on foot, and we must have food and water. Our men will fight Kaibito if they must, but there are too few of us to win. It is better that we find a distraction to draw Kaibito and his men away, and hope that the soldiers I saw with my awareness are after Kaibito. Unless we eliminate Kaibito and his men as a threat, they will hunt us down and kill us."

"You have the gifts of sorcery. Can't you confuse them and draw them away?"

"My sorcery utilizes the awareness of other beings. In this desert there are few animals big enough to be used against the enemy. Acting directly upon the awareness of man is the most difficult to deploy and can be resisted."

"My prescience tells me of death, but not the annihilation of all our people."

"Your prescience sees probabilities, the most likely outcome if one does not act, but since the future is not fixed the outcome is not certain."

Shanni remained silent, pondering Tonah's words.

"You should know of another battle being waged on another plane," Tonah continued. "At dawn I projected my awareness and saw soldiers. They may be trailing Kaibito and his men. Another awareness attacked a rider with them that I later recognized as Caleb Stone. I fear there are evil men with sorcerer's powers who see him as a threat and are working to destroy him."

"But why Caleb? He has no knowledge of such things."

"He has a powerful potential, unknown to himself. They have detected it and seek to destroy him before it develops. I should have recognized it sooner."

"I think we must fight the battle of this world first," Shanni replied. "If Kaibito succeeds in destroying us, the rest won't matter."

"I cannot argue with your logic, but many things of this world do not proceed on logic. I'm afraid it won't be so simple. The battles will go on side-by-side, and intertwined."

Tonah was right, Shanni thought, feeling despair rising inside her. Their situation was grim, but they must not give up. They had to find a way to break away from their captors.

Perplexed with their problems, the hour's walk to the cliff dwellings passed swiftly. The valley was a natural valley that spilled out of the canyon where Kaibito's camp was located. The ground rose perceptibly as they neared the sheer wall of the cliff in which the dwellings were located. The cliff dwellings were in a natural hollow in the face of the cliff far above the valley floor.

As they reached the base of the cliff, Shanni saw old stone steps worn smooth by the tread of many feet and polished by the wind. She began the tortuous climb with Tonah close behind. Their guard showed a strange reluctance to follow and stayed behind. That suited Shanni, and it was obvious they could not escape. Halfway up the cliff face the rock wall became steeper, and the steps ran out. In their place, handholds and footholds had been carved into the face of the cliff. They continued to climb upward. At last they reached the level of the cliff dwellings and stopped to catch their breath. Ghostly apartments, composed of stone and mortar rose from the plaza floor in tall, narrow column toward the overhanging roof. Blank windows and doorways broke the face of the buildings, and precipitous stairways led down to the plaza. Many more people once lived here than at Mesa Verde, Shanni thought, overwhelmed by the size of the stone city. They must have been a great people, but they too had disappeared. Had they returned to the south as the Huastecs were trying to do?

Tonah walked about, exploring the ruins. He spotted a circular kiva and called to Shanni. He climbed onto the roof and moved toward the access hole in the center. Shanni joined him as he lowered himself down the ancient wooden ladder. The interior contained prayer sticks, ritual vessels, and stone writings. All were carefully set aside as if awaiting the return of the priests to conduct services. A fine dust coated the objects that had waited centuries for their owners to return. They climbed back outside the kiva. Tonah walked to the edge to sit cross-legged, staring out across the valley to the canyons and sheer rock outcroppings leading away to the horizon to the southeast.

"I will meditate," he said, "And pray for the deliverance of our people."

Shanni left him and walked across the plaza to gaze out over the valley. She focused her gift of prescience, attempting to reach the Center, but only darkness came to her. The contact had been broken many centuries ago. Maybe the Center no longer existed.

She heard Tonah approaching and turned as he spoke. "I have renewed hope. The Huastecs have been faithful to our gods, and they will not forsake us. We must not lose faith that we will be delivered from these evil men."

"Yes. We must look until the way is opened to us."

Together they walked about the plaza, absorbing the feelings of the ancient culture. In a corner of the plaza where the depression of the cliff narrowed, Shanni saw markings in the cliff face and moved closer to investigate. She saw that handholds had been carved in the rock face, making a pathway to the top of the cliff. The ancients had carved an escape route out of the valley. Once ascended, an army could be held off below. She pointed out the carvings to Tonah, who immediately grasped their significance.

"Our faith has been rewarded. We must return and make our plans to escape."

They were silent, each lost in his thoughts, as they climbed down and walked back up the canyon to camp. Dusk had fallen and Shanni joined the young men and Tonah around the campfire, and shared what they had found. Matal and the others listened with suppressed excitement. At last they had some hope, something to provide hope. Now they could finalize a plan to escape. The time to act was now while only a few men remained in camp.

Shanni left the men to their plans and returned to her bed. With the help of the gods, her people now had a chance. Late at night a commotion awakened her. She tiptoed to the opening in the stone wall and peeked out. Noises of horses and men unloading packs reached her as she made out dim outlines moving outside. A tall form materialized out of the shadows, moving with strong strides toward the dwelling. An icy chill enveloped her as she recognized Kaibito's voice calling to Hosta.

Moments passed, marked by the tripping of her heart, when Shanni heard the footsteps approaching her room. Kaibito appeared large in the doorway, a confident smile breaking his fierce visage in the dim moonlight. Shanni realized his intent as fear and loathing swept over her.

"Go away," she whispered. "I do not want you here!"

"I will not hurt you. I had a long journey and fought hard. Now I want the comfort of my lodge and a beautiful woman. You are very beautiful, you know that, don't you?"

He reached out to caress her hair. Shanni backed away toward the wall. Kaibito's eyes lit with understanding.

"Ah, we have an inexperienced one. That's all the better. Kaibito will introduce you to your womanhood."

He reached out and forced her to him.

"Stop!" Shanni shrieked, struggling to push him away.

He overpowered her and pushed her to the floor. Shanni realized her struggling was only inflaming him. She relaxed and fought for calmness. Kaibito drew back and began removing his shirt. Shanni rose to a kneeling position and looked directly into his eyes.

"So this is the great Kaibito!" she said scornfully. "Taking maidens against their will in the middle of the night. I do not want you; you are taking me by force and I hate you for it. Is this the way the great Navaho prove their manhood?"

Kaibito snapped back as if stung, anger twisting his features. He lashed out and slapped her cruelly, knocking her onto her side. He loomed over her, fists clenched.

"Huastec slut! Kaibito is too good for the likes of you, but you will learn respect. Before I am done with your people, you will come to me on your knees and beg me to take you!"

He turned and stormed from the room. Shanni sank back against the cold, stone wall, and pulled the blanket about her. Kaibito's threat rang in her ears as she trembled silently and alone.

Chapter 8

Shanni awakened early while the camp still slept. She peered outside and saw the small vale covered with sleeping men. Kaibito had been successful in recruiting additional men. Soon he would have a small army of fighters with which to strike terror into the whites. Shanni went about her duties, her mind feverish as she conceived and then discarded plans for escape. She knew she must not delay. Soon, maybe tonight, Kaibito would return to her. She shuddered. She dreaded to be leaving the others, but staying would not help them now. She must escape to save herself and find help, even from soldiers if necessary. She finished her chores quickly and walked down to the Huastec camp where Tonah sat facing the east. His mood was somber and they sat in silence until Shanni spoke.

"Tonah, I must escape tonight. I have not told you before because I did not wish to add to your burdens, but before he left Kaibito told me I was to be his woman when he returned. Last night he came to me and I drove him away. I cannot submit to him and I must get away before he comes again. I fear that next time he will take me by force."

Tonah's eyes were tired as they met Shanni's.

"Then you must go, but I fear you will die in the desert. This is a terrible land. I will go with you."

"No, you are needed here and your strength would not withstand the desert. I will go alone and find help and then return to free the Huastecs."

Tonah reflected a moment. "The choices are not good. You must do what you must. I will pray for the gods to guide you. Meanwhile, we will prepare food and water for you. Tonight I will go with you as far as the ancient mesa. You can climb out from there and then your fate will be in the hands of the gods."

Shanni nodded. It was all they could do.

Kaibito arose late and busied himself with the affairs of the camp. He glanced at Shanni and smiled when he emerged from his dwelling. His plans were going well and he was full of confidence. He walked among the men, awakening them and getting the camp buzzing with activity.

Shanni planned throughout the day. She ate well and put aside dried food to pack away when she left camp. She fought down the fear that welled up when she thought of what she must do. She forced the fear aside to focus and believe that she would succeed. When night fell and the evening meal had been completed, Shanni picked up empty water gourds and walked to the water basin. Her passage went unnoticed in the general activity of the camp. She slipped the pack of dried food to Tonah and he nodded. The food and water bag would be ready when she came for them.

Kaibito was with his men at the fire, conversing noisily. Laughter pealed out and Shanni saw that they were drinking, no doubt celebrating their successful trip. Later Kaibito would come for her and the drink would make him unpredictable.

She returned to the dwelling, ignoring Hosta's hostile glare. She went to her pallet and pulled the crude blanket over her as if to sleep. She heard Hosta padding about in the next room and then quieting down to sleep. Occasional sounds reached her from the campfire. The men were celebrating late, which helped her plans.

She arose and made her way to the opening in the wall that served as a window. She climbed through and clung to the shadows as she circled the camp and reached the area near the pool of water. Tonah appeared noiselessly and without a word led away hugging the shadows of the canyon wall. Shanni knew that lookouts guarded the entrance to the canyon, but they were well hidden and she did not see them. She felt her pulse beating in her throat as she followed Tonah in the moonless night. Only the stars lit their passage as they moved carefully to avoid noise on the rocky ground. In order to keep hidden in the shadows of the canyon walls, they could not go directly across the valley to the ancient mesa. Their route was circuitous and hours passed before they saw the ghostly dwellings in the face of the cliff. Shanni shuddered, and looked up at the sheer wall in the dim light. She must climb that wall clinging to the faint hand and foot holds carved into the face of the cliff.

Tonah embraced her tightly for a moment. "The gods direct your path, Shanni."

She nodded and turned to begin the tortuous climb. Tonah stood watching a moment and then he was gone. He must be back in camp before Shanni's escape was discovered. The climb was arduous in the dark. Shanni had to feel carefully for each hold. Occasionally her grasp would slip, but she kept her feet firmly planted as she climbed to reach the plaza of the ancient dwellings. She paused on the plaza to catch her breath. All was still in the shadows. She turned and made her way to the end of the plaza where it merged into the sheer cliff wall. A sudden whirr of wings startled her until she realized a bat had been disturbed as she moved by. She felt along the rock wall with her fingers, trying to locate the handholds carved into the cliff face. She had to stretch out from her narrow perch over the canyon lying far below. Her water bag, secured to her shoulder by a leather strap, shifted and she teetered, grasping at the stone face. Her fingers found a handhold and then her toes, feeling through her moccasins, found a slot. A cool breeze whipped at her clothing as she climbed, pausing frequently for breath. A pale moon rose in the east, lighting the valley floor and casting shadows on the face of the cliff where Shanni clung, a tiny speck in the vastness. Hours passed as she made slow progress. The cliff started to tilt away as she neared the top, relieving some of the pressure as she climbed, but the stone face had weathered over the centuries so that the hand and foot holds were shallow and difficult to use. Shanni felt a stab of panic. What if they disappeared before she reached the top? She could never climb back down. She looked up at the top of the mesa, tantalizingly close. She heaved a sigh of relief as the holds continued and she completed the last few steps to the top. She lay gasping for breath as the moon reached its zenith, lighting the mesa and the surrounding country. She climbed to her feet and looked about. Rugged mountains and harsh canyons met her gaze as she turned, looking for a likely path to follow. The mesa on which she stood led away to the east and narrowed into a ridge that led down into a canyon. She began walking in that direction.

It was late at night when Kaibito left the celebration at the campfire. The trip had been successful and he was recruiting more men as his fame grew throughout the region. Despite the strong drink, his gait was steady as he walked up the gentle rise to his dwelling. Flushed with success, his thoughts turned to Shanni. Tonight would be the appropriate time to make her his woman. She would join the great war chief Kaibito!

He eased into the small room where Shanni slept and bent over her pallet in the dim light. He reached out to touch her and realized she was not there! Perhaps she had heard him approaching and was hiding. He peered about but could not find her. He moved to the other room and rudely awakened Hosta, demanding the whereabouts of the slave girl.

"I do not know," Hosta whined, "She was sleeping when I went to bed."

"Find her!" Kaibito roared. The slave girl dared to try to escape Kaibito? She would come to him begging on her knees!

He raised the alarm and his men scattered drunkenly. He realized that they would accomplish little before dawn. He swept through the camp of the Huastecs. No one else was missing. He questioned the old man Tonah whom he awakened from a sound sleep. Tonah appeared befuddled and offered no help.

Kaibito swallowed his anger with an effort. She would not get far in the desert. Tomorrow his trackers would find her and bring her back and then he would handle her.

Chapter 9

The sun had passed the zenith when Caleb saw the lead rider pause and scan the horizon expectantly. A man's silhouette appeared near the rim of the canyon and waved them on. Caleb's hands were raw from the bindings that held him to the saddle horn. Two days had passed since the ambush and he guessed they were nearing their destination.

They emerged from a narrow canyon to cross a broad valley remarkable for the ruins of the cliff dwelling set high in the wall that closed off exit to the north. They turned off into a smaller canyon that soon led to a sizeable camp filled with grazing horses, crude dwellings and people bustling about. Caleb felt his tension rising. This must be Kaibito's camp and he recalled Manuelito's comments. Kaibito was capable of killing him on the spot. He'd have to find a way to delay Kaibito until he could devise a means to escape.

As they approached the camp, a stocky Indian stood up from the campfire and hailed the leader, Laga.

"We expected you earlier. We began to worry."

"We ran into bluecoats," Laga answered. "We killed some and we brought this one, who rode with them, for Kaibito."

"Kaibito is not in camp. He and the riders are hunting a slave who escaped."

"Very well. We're tired and this one can wait. Put him with the others and guard him well."

Rough hands untied Caleb and pulled him from the saddle. He was retied and seated alone near a campfire site located adjacent to the water basin. His wrists throbbed from the coarse rope and he changed position trying to ease the discomfort. The sun had sunk behind the west wall of the canyon when Caleb saw the figures of men walking down the canyon toward the camp. In the shadows he could not make out their features. He saw riders with rifles following and knew these were Kaibito's captives returning to camp.

As they approached Caleb saw a stooped figure that appeared familiar. As the man emerged from the shadows, he saw white hair framing a lined face and recognized Tonah. So Kaibito had captured the Huastecs. Where was Shanni? Caleb looked but did not recognize her among the women returning to camp

. The Huastecs were tired and plodded unseeing into camp to sit wearily near the campsite. Tonah looked in Caleb's direction and his eyes lit with recognition. Somehow Tonah did not seem surprised. Had he sensed Caleb's presence? Tonah looked away and sat lost in thought, giving no sign of recognition to the guards. Darkness fell quickly. One of the guards untied Caleb for him to eat and drink, and then bound him again for the night. He was given a blanket and found a spot in the shadows to bed down for the night. The guard sat leaning against a rock, smoking and watching the campsite. Quiet settled over the camp as the tired Huastecs fell asleep.

Caleb was dozing when he felt a slight nudge and tilted his head to hear a low whisper from the shadows. "It's Tonah. Do not move or the guard will see us. How do you come to be here?"

The guard was nodding off and Caleb risked worming deeper into the shadows. He sat up to face Tonah.

"I was riding with soldiers who were hunting Kaibito. We were ambushed and I was captured."

"How close are the soldiers? Can they help us?"

"Not likely. We were two days' ride to the east. They may have regrouped by now and started to follow."

"The danger increases for us here with each passing day. We cannot overcome Kaibito's men without help."

"Where is Shanni?"

"She ran away into the desert. Kaibito had taken her to his household and was going to make her his woman. He and his riders are out searching for her now."

"My God! She'll die out there alone!"

"I fear for her also, but she would not stay and submit to Kaibito. I could not abandon the others and go with her."

"I must find her, and soon."

"I know. I brought you a knife. It is not much of a weapon, but it is all that was not taken from us."

Tonah sawed at the rope and Caleb felt his bonds give way. Tonah placed a rusty clasp knife in Caleb's hand and eased away to his bed.

Caleb flexed his hands to restore circulation while he watched the guard doze. He needed a rifle and a horse. He tested the short blade of the knife and set his jaw. It wasn't much to stake his life on but it would have to do. He began to edge toward the guard.

Chapter 10

Lieutenant Porter rubbed his shoulder and listened to the scout's earnest discourse. The troop had been lucky, all things considered. They had taken casualties in the first volley, but had been able to retreat down-canyon before their attackers could cut them off. Then unexpectedly the attackers had broken off and fled to the south, which prompted the present discussion.

"The trail has led northwest for days. The attack was a diversion." Manuelito's scout, Raza, was speaking. "We must be closing on Kaibito's camp and they're trying to lead us in a different direction. I say we continue toward the northwest."

Porter nodded. It made sense. He was not a scholar but he knew Indian fighting. They would've been cut to ribbons if the ambush had been set up properly. The attack had been hasty, and with too few men. Likely it was a small party of Kaibito's men. There was a way to find out if the retreat was a diversion.

"Raza, you take two men and follow their trail. Be careful not to overtake them and fall into another ambush. Go only far enough to see if their trail circles back north. Meanwhile I'll lead the main troop northwest. If they head off, don't try to follow. Hightail it back and join us."

Raza nodded, and led two men out of sight up the canyon.

Porter turned to the men. "Smith, I figure we're due north of Fort Defiance. If we find ol' Kaibito's den, we'll likely need help in flushing him out. You ride to the Fort and alert them. Tell them we'll use the heliograph to signal if we find Kaibito."

With a nod, Smith mounted his horse and rode away.

"Now, men," Porter drawled, "Look sharp, for the price of poker is about to go up!"

Kaibito paced to and fro in front of the campfire. He had returned at dusk leaving his scouts to continue the search for the woman. He had been anxious to hear Laga's report, and the news was not good. The bluecoats had not been diverted. Kaibito's men could handle the soldiers, but Laga had seen a rider detach from the troop and ride south. That rider would be striking for Fort Defiance for reinforcements and that created a real threat.

He gave orders for his men to take positions in the narrow canyon leading to the valley. They could hold the troop off indefinitely there. Meanwhile, he would prepare the camp for a quick retreat if it came to that. Perhaps reinforcements would not come, or maybe the bluecoats would not find the entrance to the canyon.

"What about the white captive?" Laga asked.

Kaibito paused. He had not forgotten the man who had killed his warriors. He would kill him but it would not be quick. He had no time for it now.

"Let him wait. We will kill him at our leisure after we deal with the bluecoats."

Laga nodded and grinned. He knew what Kaibito had in mind.

Kaibito's thoughts returned to the slave girl. He was angry that she had not been found, but she was unimportant. It would serve her right to die of thirst on the desert. He had deigned to treat her well and she had been ungrateful. Let her suffer the consequences. He would pull back his scouts and seal her fate. Kaibito smiled as he gave the order.

Caleb felt the dull knife blade with his thumb as he crept forward. It would not do. Instead, he grasped a fist-sized rock and leaped forward to strike the guard a solid blow. Caleb grabbed the guard's rifle as he crumpled to the ground, and then hugged the shadows as he moved away to search for a horse.

A dark shape loomed in his path. "Who is there?"

Caleb swung the rifle barrel in a savage arc, smashing the rider from the saddle without a sound. Caleb grabbed the reins and swung astride the horse.

Rifles opened up, sending bullets streaking by him in the cold air. The way south was blocked; he'd have to gamble on finding a way out up the canyon. He spurred the horse around a corner, scanning the ancient gullies that broke the sheer canyon wall.

He heard his pursuers closing and chose a ravine at random, fighting the horse over the uneven ground. He rounded the corner and the ravine abruptly ended in a box canyon. He was trapped! He abandoned the horse and scrambled through the broken rocks on foot.

He paused to send a barrage of rifle shots down the ravine, breaking the charge of his pursuers. He could hear them scrambling back around the corner to avoid the direct line of fire.

Caleb found a crack in the rock and climbed, looking for a way out. His pursuers had braved the corner and he could hear them closing on foot. He climbed until he reached the top of the wall and crawled over out of sight. Bullets careened off the rocks but he was clear. They would be cautious about attempting the climb in the dark with him waiting in ambush, but he did not intend to wait. There were enough to surround him if he tried to hold them off.

The darkness worked in his favor as he concentrated on gaining distance. He moved quickly and soon the sound of pursuit faded. They would be after him again come morning, but he meant to be far from here, leaving no trail on the rocky ground.

He took his direction from the stars and circled until he faced east. He walked until he found a likely niche to rest until morning. Then he must find Shanni.

Chapter 11

The farmer Ramon Pima watched with a mixture of familiarity and caution as the slight form of Jorge Tupac walk down the gravelly path toward him. Jorge was a mysterious, wizened old man who traveled from village to village selling a few items and doing odd jobs. People found Jorge's behavior eccentric. His speech would ramble good-naturedly and he would contradict himself without being aware of it. Some thought he spent too much time alone while others said that the sun had cooked his brain.

But he was harmless enough, Ramon thought, and he brought the news. He would do a few chores, entertain the children, and after a few days he would move on. Neither Ramon nor the others suspected that Jorge Tupac was the most dangerous man in northern Mexico.

"Ah, Jorge, it is good to see you." Ramon greeted. "You will eat and stay with us for the night."

Jorge pulled up and smiled foolishly. "I appreciate your offer, Ramon. I have walked a long way today, too far for the legs of an old man, but I regret I cannot stay. I must keep moving."

Ramon's surprise showed. "But Jorge, you always stay a few days. Surely your business cannot be so urgent."

"I know, my friend, and I always look forward to your hospitality. Another time, perhaps."

Jorge seemed preoccupied, Ramon thought. Was he ill?

Jorge watered the burro, filled his canteen and then moved on, muttering to himself.

Ramon shook his head and watched Jorge climb toward the foothills.

Near sunset, Jorge stopped and made camp for the night. He built a campfire and prepared a simple meal. After eating, he pulled a pipe out of his saddlebags. He stoked the pipe with ingredients from the medicine bag around his neck and used a coal from the fire to light it. He settled back, leaning against a rock and drew a long draft from the pipe. The smoke curled around him as he exhaled. He relaxed, watching the firelight flicker over the coals, and projected his awareness.

There was the moment of shimmering as the world disappeared and he reappeared at the top of a stone pyramid, wearing the clothes of a priest. Other priests sat in the circle, watching him expectantly, as he spoke.

"The disturbance in the node was real. Even now, people travel toward us in the everyday world who know how to influence the matrix."

One of the priests spoke, "We were warned when the Center took control that all the adepts might not have been destroyed, but who could have predicted that they would surface again after all these years!"

"The question is what to do," another offered.

"One of them already has full skill and knowledge," Jorge continued. "He has projected his awareness and found me. I sense that others in his group may have the potential, but have not yet developed it. We must stop them before they become aware of their ability to work against us as a combined force."

"What do you suggest?"

Jorge turned, looking down from the heights of the pyramid to the broad plaza below. Hundreds of people stood silently, their faces lit by torches as they gazed up at the priests framed by the stars overhead. Jorge felt sadness as he realized that once the people were real, gathered by the tens of thousands in the plaza of the everyday world. Now they only existed in the dimension where time stood still, the world of the awareness.

"They travel to us in the world of men; in that world we will stop them."

"That will be difficult," another priest said. "There are few resources we can use against them in the place where they travel."

"I have selected a type of predator, a killing machine that already lives in the desert. We will join our awareness to force the predators to do our bidding. We will set them upon our enemies to destroy them."

"So shall it be," the priest said as the others nodded agreement.

Shanni awakened from her cramped position and blinked drowsily in the fresh sunlight. A day had passed and she was hopelessly lost. She had found a hidden niche under a rock and waited until Kaibito's riders had disappeared to search elsewhere. She stared at a solitary cactus that had somehow found a foothold in the rocky terrain. A solitary red bloom opened to the sun, a spot of beauty breaking the barren landscape. As she watched, a tiny flicker of movement caught her eye and she saw a spider finishing its web in front of the flower. Minutes passed as the spider withdrew, waiting. She heard the drone of a bee approaching and watched it enter the bloom, working busily to remove the nectar. As it lifted to fly away, it became entangled in the web and struggled frantically to break away. The spider reappeared and moved swiftly to the bee. It sank fangs deep into the bee's body and it became still in death. The spider ate greedily, sucking the body fluids out of the bee, leaving a desiccated husk.

Shanni shuddered. Even the beauty of the desert was a snare where life hung precariously and death came suddenly to the unwary. She peered out from her hiding place. Although his riders had gone away, she could not be far from his camp and she stood no chance in the open against mounted riders.

She would have to travel at night and stay hidden during the day. She was thirsty, and tried to drink sparingly from her water. Even so, it would not last another day. She had to get away and to find water.

The day passed slowly as she dozed in the dry heat. At sunset, she awakened as the desert began to cool. She gathered the food and water bag and picked her way along the rocky slope, avoiding the sand that would leave sign of her passage. She kept to the shadows as she moved, and paused as she heard a dry buzz and froze as the sidewinder moved away a few feet from where she stood. She realized the enormity of her peril steeled herself and continued.

A full moon rose, lighting her path in the night, casting a surreal landscape of grays and shadows. She entered a narrow canyon and the walking became easier on the hard gravel. Near morning she looked for a place to hide for the day, but the canyon wall was smooth, without a break, and she quickened her pace to find shelter.

She heard a faint sound and shrank back into the shadows, listening. She recognized the soft footsteps of a horse walking and the occasional squeak of saddle leather. Had one of Kaibito's riders circled back? She felt her pulse pounding in her ears as she waited. The sound died away in the desert stillness and she let out her breath.

She continued down the canyon until it branched into a wider canyon broken by steep ravines and ghostly shadows in the dim light of daybreak. She found a gully and climbed up the broken wash to a sheltered nook where she settled down to await the dawn.

Hours had passed when she awakened to bright sunlight filling the niche. She had to get her bearings before traveling any further. She crept out of her hiding place and moved down the dry wash to the intersection with the canyon. She gazed down the canyon as it widened into a long stretch of broken desert, with only a few rounded hills to the east. Walking would be easier, but she would be visible for miles. She would have to cross it in one night or risk being caught out in daylight with no place to hide.

She turned to return to her hiding place when a slight depression in the sand caught her attention. She moved closer and made out the faint print of a boot. Someone had passed by on foot. Had one of the Huastecs escaped? Not likely, as most of them wore moccasins, and Kaibito's men would be mounted. She would have to redouble her vigilance. Was she to escape one enemy to fall into the hands of another? She returned to the niche to wait out the day.

It was the ultimate killing machine. Self-contained and mobile, its sole reason for being was to take life efficiently and remorselessly. Sampling the air as it moved, it could detect odors as small as a part per million and move without sound over rough terrain. It could set up and arm itself and lay in wait until a life form came into range. It was unaware of time, and would wait patiently for hours or even days until time to act.

In total darkness, it could detect a living creature's body heat, measuring and recording temperature variations of one-thirtieth of a degree Fahrenheit. Its decision center computed the target's trajectory, size, speed and range and instantly determined the precise type, quantity and mixture of deadly toxin to deliver.

In less than half a second, it could drive forward and deliver a lethal cocktail of chemical compounds composed primarily of proteins, proteolytic enzymes, and polypeptides of low molecular weight, setting in motion the devastating breakdown of a living organism's system.

The delivery system consisted of dual cylinders, independently activated, with replacement injectors in standby positions. Damaged cylinders were replaced automatically without detracting from functionality or lethality.

After the attack, the killing machine retracted and rearmed, the ultimate in stealth, motionless and undetectable. The target of the attack reacted violently, convulsed, and then attempted to flee as its circulatory and lymphatic system pumped the deadly toxin throughout its body. Each of the twenty-five proteins in the toxin attacked a part of the body, causing hemorrhage, breakdown of nucleic acids, and organ failure. A group of enzymes began the process of digesting the body from the inside, causing neurological failure. Within seconds the body's defense systems were ravished and the victim lay paralyzed, suffocating, dying.

The killing machine waited patiently. Its brain had already computed the size and quantity of its target. If the target was prey, the rattlesnake would follow its odor trail and consume the body whole. Otherwise, it would abandon its victim and leisurely move away without fear or remorse, for it was the ultimate predator: it existed only to kill.

At dusk the rattlesnakes stirred from the den and moved forth, each to find its feeding spot for the night. They followed the instinct instilled by six million years of evolution and the homing pattern that kept them within the immediate area of their birth for life.

This night a powerful force moved over them, without their knowledge or awareness. The force overrode their normal patterns and they moved forward as a unit, crawling westward into uncharted territory.

The moon was rising in the east when Shanni reached the end of the canyon to gaze out over the desert. She waited long

minutes, watching and listening for signs of movement. Nothing
stirred and she knew the time had come.

She stepped out briskly, feeling vulnerable in the open
moonlight. The only sound was a low breeze that moved across
the dessert, sending a chill down her spine. Her pulse beat in her
throat and she pulled the shawl close about her in the sudden
chill as she stepped out from the safety of the rocks.

The moon climbed higher and Shanni paused to look back at
the canyon wall, looming above the horizon, miles away. She
was committed, now she must get across the plain before
daylight. She turned and continued her progress. The walking
became easier as the ground tilted down into a broad bowl-like
depression in the desert floor. A few low rock outcroppings
broke the gravelly desert floor.

She perceived a flicker of movement ahead and froze in her
tracks, sinking quickly to the ground to wait, breathless. She
realized with horror that rattlesnakes, undulating in unison, were
moving directly toward her.

TONAH LAY QUIETLY by the campfire as the others slept. He
gazed unseeing at the stars overhead, his awareness centered on
his intuition. A chill swept over him as he felt a dread, a
premonition of peril. He gathered his energy and began the
process of projecting his awareness.

His awareness rose high over the canyons and found a night
owl, sitting on a ledge, preparing to launch itself out over the
wide plain to hunt prey in the moonlight. Its eyes were
telescopic, adapted to detecting the tiniest movement in the vast
landscape. As it soared over the landscape, a curious movement
on the gravelly earth caught its attention. It swooped lower to
investigate, and then broke off to climb as it recognized the
movement was not of prey, but of danger. Tonah recoiled as his
awareness recognized the abnormal and deadly migration of
rattlesnakes across the desert floor. To be moving so was alien to
their nature. They should not be there. And he felt a presence
nearby that he recognized as Shanni.

Tonah released the owl and returned awareness to the campfire. He crawled to where Aurel was sleeping and awakened his with a nudge.

"Awaken Matal and follow me," he whispered. "Terror awaits. There is no time to lose!"

They convened in the shadows and Tonah related what he had seen. "Only a group of sorcerers has the power to move animals in unison. I must draw on your strength to break their hold on the rattlesnakes. Shanni is in danger and there is little time."

"But I am not trained at that level," Aurel said. "And Matal pursues the warrior's path in the everyday world. How can we help you?"

"You must trust me completely. I will engage the awareness of each of you and take you along with me. You will experience surprise and terror, but must remain strong. Ignore your feelings and let the terror slide over you like water. Above all, you must project your resolve in support of my will."

"Will it be enough? There may be many of them," Matal said.

"We are all we have. It will have to do."

Matal closed his eyes and attempted to quiet his mind, despite his racing thoughts. Tonight he envied Aurel who had practiced the arts while he had focused on learning the use of weapons. His nature did not turn to introspection; he had no patience for it.

He felt drowsy and his breathing slowed. As if in a dream, he saw Tonah and Aurel standing before him, and Tonah motioned him to join them. He got up and walked to Tonah, who placed his hand on his shoulder. A feeling of pride, of affection, flowed over Matal and he realized he wanted to please Tonah, to help him at whatever cost. Aurel reached out and placed his hand on Matal's other shoulder, and he felt himself soaring, flowing with Aurel, following Tonah's awareness. He concentrated on believing that this could be happening.

They were in total darkness. Matal felt fear and dread permeating an unworldly place. He fought down panic. What had happened to Aurel and Tonah? Had he been abandoned? He remembered Tonah's warning and focused on trusting. He felt himself calming, and then he "felt" Tonah's voice communicating in the void.

"I seek a guardian."

"Many seek. Few find. Who are you?"

"My worldly name is 'Tonah'."

"What guardian do you seek?"

"The guardian of the peccary."

"Few seek him."

"Few know of his strength."

"True. As you wish, then."

Matal saw the dim outlines of Tonah and Aurel appear in front of him. He reached out with his awareness and placed his "hand" on Aurel's shoulder. He felt confidence returning.

The void shimmered in front of them, and a huge form manifested out of the void. As it solidified, Matal felt terror as the giant snout of a peccary reached out to them, lethal incisors set to rip and maim. The black snout was covered with bristles that faded into a satin black coat that covered the face, leaving only burning eyes staring down at them. Matal recoiled as the nightmare emerged and wished it to end.

"Steady." Matal felt Tonah's voice in his awareness. "Ignore your feelings; let them flow over you like water."

"You summoned me. What do you want?" the apparition said.

"We seek your help against those who attempt to do us harm." Tonah replied.

"Why should I help you?"

"Because I invoke it against the powers of evil."

"How do I know you are not the evildoer?"

"Because I can show you what we face."

"Show me, then."

Matal felt Tonah's awareness expand, outlining a vast plain on the blackness of the void. The full moon in a night sky lit the landscape of a broad plain, and on that plain the eyes of an owl saw the motion of reptiles, crawling in unison, intent on a purpose. Tonah's awareness shifted and Matal felt terror sweeping over him in waves as he experienced what Tonah "saw" as the still form of Shanni below.

Awareness faded and they returned to the peccary.

"It is as you say. I will help you. I will break the attack, but you must overcome the attackers. They are from your world, not mine."

"I understand. Before we engage them, we will need an anchor, a beacon for our return to the ordinary world of men."

"It will be as you request."

The entity began to fade from view as a pinpoint of light appeared. The light expanded into an acorn that tumbled down, engaging their attention as it fell to ground under the shade of oaks along a river. The air was cool as a herd of peccaries grazed peacefully on the acorns, while piglets scampered in the morning sun. A sense of peace and tranquility spread over Matal. This was the meaning of life. He felt warm and comfortable, with an urge to weep with joy.

"This is the beacon," Tonah said. "Remember it with your feelings, for we must come this way again."

Matal's awareness was jerked away and he found himself in the void, a sense of movement whirling about him, disorienting and vague. He reached out instinctively. He felt Tonah's hand on his shoulder as they looked down at the plain.

A herd of peccaries appeared from the rocks and began trotting toward the gravelly plain. Sensing their direction, they began grunting in anger, working into a frenzied run as they tore across the plain toward the rattlesnakes.

The rattlesnakes did not know fear, but they instinctively recognized death. The peccary had evolved immunity to the rattlesnake's bite, and routinely killed them as they competed for space. Where peccaries roamed, rattlesnakes died. It had been so for thousands of years.

The lead snakes automatically tested the air as they advanced and suddenly detected a new and deadly odor. Six million years of evolution had programmed the snake to retreat at all costs beyond the peccary's reach in order to survive. Each rattlesnake's survival mechanism rebelled against the force that was propelling it forward, and the snakes began to writhe in chaos.

The sudden backlash to the force caused a backup of energy, creating an overload that surged like a river back along the projected awareness. The overload was the instant Tonah had been waiting for. He took advantage of the chaos to drive his full intent along the surge, following the projection to its source.

Matal was swept madly along with Tonah and Aurel, tumbling end over end through the void. He was everywhere and nowhere. They "landed" and the scene snapped into place. They were standing on a stone pyramid lit by torches and starlight. A dozen men, in the robes of priests, stood with eyes closed as if in a trance, concentrating.

It appeared that the men were not aware of their presence, Matal thought, and then one of the priests opened his eyes as awareness returned.

A shriek filled the air as the priest exploded into a giant rattlesnake, poised to strike. Matal, terrorized, shrank back as Tonah shouted for the guardian. Tonah morphed into a giant peccary and began pawing at the rattlesnake with powerful hooves, squeals of anger rending the air. The other priests awoke, and the rattlesnake became bigger and stronger, towering over the peccary that was Tonah.

Matal felt Tonah's call for strength, and looked at Aurel, who was standing with eyes closed. Matal forced himself to close his eyes and felt the tug of Tonah's life force. He let go and went with the flow. The peccary grew stronger and seized the rattlesnake in its snout. It bit down and Matal felt a shriek of anger and fear. Matal opened his eyes. The rattlesnake had disappeared and Tonah stood before him. Tonah reached out, staggering, as Aurel moved to steady him.

"Quickly," Tonah said. "We must return before our strength is gone."

"Think of the beacon," Aurel shouted to Matal. "Remember your feelings so it can draw us back!"

Matal recalled the center of peace within this world of terror. He wanted to be there. He wanted more than anything to go home.

He felt the disorientation and the sense of movement return. Again he was alone and frightened in the void. He was falling through space, tumbling out of control until he landed gently in the glade. The peccaries continued to graze, unaware of his presence. Matal felt a sense of gratitude and peace. He started to relax and let go.

"No!" the awareness of Aurel reached him. "This is the beacon. You must not stay here."

"But I like it here," Matal felt himself protesting. "This way is peace."

"That way is death," Tonah interrupted. "You must not hold on to your emotions. Let them go. They will trap you here."

Reluctantly Matal answered Tonah's strong call and willed himself to follow Tonah. The scene wavered and disappeared and he felt the cold ground of the canyon beneath him. He looked about as Aurel placed wood on the fire and wrapped Tonah, who lay still as death, in a blanket.

Shanni felt the air stir around her as the snakes approached and she turned to flee. She tripped in the darkness and went down, rolling as the first rattlesnake approached and terror enveloped her.

Suddenly she felt a strong disturbance in the air, like a dust storm, swirling over her. The snakes stopped. She watched in horrid fascination as the snakes broke ranks and turned, scrambling away in confusion.

Shanni sank back as fear and loathing gave way to exhaustion. She felt the presence of Tonah. Somehow he had intervened. How she wished he were here with her.

Shanni looked at the edge of the plain, too far away. She had lost valuable time, and she was exhausted. The moon went behind a cloud, darkening her surroundings. She was terrified to take a step she could not see with rattlesnakes about, and she could not make it to shelter before daybreak. She would be caught out in the plain at daybreak. She must find a place to wait out the daylight hours.

In the dim moonlight, she saw the shadowy outline of a man walking toward her. Was she hallucinating? She shrank back, looking for a place to hide. As the form continued, she realized he was moving away from her. There was something vaguely familiar about the way he walked. Had he escaped from Kaibito also?

A low sound of hoof beats signaled a rider approaching in the distance. She rose and began to walk in the direction the man had gone. She fought down her fear, putting one foot in front of the other, walking swiftly. She feared the snakes but she dared not stop. Had she imagined the sound in the night?

She turned and saw the rider silhouetted in the distance, advancing at a steady trot and barely discernable as he topped a rise in the horizon.

Shanni looked around for a place of concealment. If the rider saw her he would ride her down!

As she crouched and began to run, a shadow rose from the desert floor and dragged her down. She started to scream when a rough hand clasped her mouth.

"Don't make a sound or we're both dead."

She was lost in a surge of emotion as she recognized the voice.

"Caleb, it's you," she whispered. Caleb was intent on the approaching rider as he hugged her to him. She felt the hammering of his heart and saw the worry in his eyes.

"Thank God I found you," he said. "I must kill this one, and there may be others."

She nodded, understanding. The man could not be allowed to escape and bring others.

The rider was closing, leaning over the saddle and scanning for tracks as he advanced. The horse snorted and stopped suddenly, sensing their presence. The rider was almost unseated as Caleb moved swiftly, swinging the rifle barrel in a wide arc that clubbed the rider from the saddle.

Caleb grabbed the reins and was almost pulled off his feet as the horse shied backwards. He quieted the horse as Shanni joined him, and checked the fallen rider. Shanni recoiled at the dark pool of blood soaking into the dry sand.

"We must go. There may be others." Caleb mounted the horse and swung her up behind him.

They skimmed over the desert at a fast gallop, racing for the hills to the east. A cool wind whipped Shanni's hair as she clung to Caleb and began to lose strength as the fear and adrenaline began to drain out of her.

They gained the hills and Caleb swung around, scanning the horizon for signs of pursuit. Nothing stirred across the plain.

"Looks like he was the only one out this way," he said. "But they'll miss him come morning, and backtrack him and us. We have to keep moving, but I reckon I'll take a minute for us. Are you all right?"

He dismounted and lifted Shanni down from the horse. He held her to him, holding her long moments as if to assure she was real. After the months of worry and searching he had found her.

Shanni sighed, abandoning herself to the moment. Whatever the desert held now, she would face it with Caleb.

Chapter 12

Ramon Pima wiped sleep from his eyes as he walked out of his adobe dwelling to fetch water. Sunlight bounced off the low hills creating a prism of color as he looked up. He squinted against the glare of the sun and saw Jorge's burro silhouetted in the distance.

Ramon blinked and began to walk up the winding path. As he drew near, he saw Jorge Tupac lying motionless in the dust. Ramon scrambled to the still body and lifted Jorge's head. He was barely breathing. Ramon shouted to his wife as he carried Jorge down the hill. He placed Jorge on a cot in the coolness of the dwelling as his wife brought water and placed a cool compress on Jorge's head. Jorge stirred and drank the offered water greedily.

"What happened?" Ramon asked. "Did you fall?"

Jorge lay back, gathering his strength to speak in a whisper. "No matter. Please let me sleep. I will need food and water when I awaken. I'll explain then. Thank you, my friends."

Jorge lapsed into unconsciousness, leaving Ramon to shake his head in wonder. Jorge had seemed so light, like a small child, when he carried him, and there was the faint aroma of singed hair. Had Jorge fallen into his campfire?

Ramon stood up and shrugged to his wife. "We'll let him rest. What else can we do?"

CALEB'S EYES SMARTED from lack of sleep as he gazed back along the trail. The morning sun, low in the east, was already washing out the colors of the desert into a slate gray. He needed rest, Caleb realized, as he blinked to focus in the shimmering heat. Presently he made out dark specks circling in the sky to the west. The vultures had found the rider he left behind last night. Those birds were signals that Kaibito's men would not fail to note. Even now riders might be picking up his trail.

Caleb turned and walked down from the knoll. Shanni was huddled, asleep, in the sparse shade of a boulder. The horse stood head down, motionless. The horse was done in, tired, yet their lives depended on it. Caleb surveyed his surroundings. There was no prospect of water or grass for the horse here. They would have to keep moving.

Caleb's vision swam and he had trouble concentrating, too much was happening too quickly. He sought the shade next to Shanni and sat down. He would let her sleep a little longer, and then they must push on. His head drooped and his eyes closed. He did not realize when he fell asleep.

Caleb snapped awake, every sense alert. How long had he slept? He looked at the sun, high in the morning sky. Hours had passed. He awakened Shanni and caught up the reins of the horse. Despite her weak protest, he lifted her to the back of the horse and began walking. The land was a mass of shallow gullies walled by low hills. He could not see far in any direction. Perfect ambush country, he thought.

He trudged doggedly in the oppressive heat until they reached the hills and Caleb found a place to leave Shanni and the horse in the shade. He climbed a rise in the land to survey their back trail. Movement caught his eye and he made out riders approaching, less than an hour's ride away. Caleb returned to Shanni. He had no choice now. He could not hide the horse's trail and the tired horse could not carry them fast enough to get away. He was gambling with their lives, he thought, as he looped the reins over the horse's neck and loosened a saddle strap to tap the horse as it walked. With luck it would keep the horse walking for hours. He led the horse out and herded it to the east.

He and Shanni followed until it crossed a rocky area where Caleb led away up a broken outcropping to the low rim of the ledge. They had to keep moving until darkness stopped the riders for the night.

At dusk, he sought out a hidden niche and they stopped for the night. They finished the food Shanni had packed, washed down with tepid water in Caleb's water bag. Tomorrow they must find water.

"I had given up hope of our finding one another again," Shanni said as she leaned back tiredly against a boulder. "We had no idea that the land is so vast and so hostile."

"Yes, the land goes on for hundreds of days' walk. We've only started."

"I was afraid you had been killed."

"I caught up with Inman and he's dead."

Shanni moved nearer and Caleb placed his arm about her. She realized the Huastecs had been sheltered from much of the violence of the outside world. Now she saw the harshness of that world and the violence of evil men. Caleb had been forced to kill to survive. Could she learn to kill? She recoiled at the thought, but somewhere to the west her people were caught in the web of a madman. To save them she would have to change. She would have to do things abhorrent to her, things that could not be taken back. She shuddered. Her world had changed. She would never be able to return to the simple life of Mesa Verde.

All she wanted now was to be with Caleb, and for them to live. The tension of the day drained out of her and she slept in Caleb's arms.

Kaibito and his men had been distracted by the hunt for Shanni, leaving Aurel alone to tend to Tonah. He was worried as he sat by and watched Tonah sleep. Tonah had been unconscious all day, breathing shallowly. Aurel had never seen him so pale and near death. Tonah had stirred, hours ago, to drink and then lapse back into unconsciousness.

Matal complained of a bad headache and swore he'd had enough of shamanism. From now on, he vowed to fight with only with guns.

Aurel experienced bouts of queasiness and brief periods when the world shimmered, but he expected it. His apprenticeship with Tonah had prepared him for aftershocks, but he'd never experienced such conflict and terror before. They had entered a new and terrible world, both within and without, and he knew that they could perish in either. Only Tonah stood between the Huastecs and disaster.

Late in the afternoon Tonah awakened and sat up. He drank more water and began eating the food Aurel brought. He seemed preoccupied, almost brooding as Aurel waited silently.

Tonah finished eating and turned to Aurel.

"Please ask Matal to join us."

Aurel left and soon returned with Matal.

"What you saw is a new and dangerous development," Tonah said. "In addition to the dangers of the everyday world, there are those who are fighting us in the world of sorcery. We will have to defend ourselves in both."

Matal looked worried. "I do not know that world. Why did you take me along? I thought I was going to die!"

"You and Aurel have the inherent strength of youth. Although you do not know how to use it, I could channel your strength in the netherworld. Even so, we were almost overcome. I am getting old. My knowledge and experience cannot offset my waning strength as I find that we are up against formidable enemies."

"But I've seen you channel the power of the universe many times," Aurel protested. "I thought that it replenished your strength like it cured Caleb."

"It is true that I've used the power to prolong my life far longer than that of ordinary men, but there is a limit. Life is the ultimate orderliness imposed upon a universe that creates and dissipates energy. Enormous energy had to be compressed and held together to make the everyday world that enables our bodies to live. Great energy is required to maintain our life, which is why we eat and sleep. Eventually the energy requirement becomes too great, and every "thing" descends from order to disorder, from complex to simple. Everything breaks down. We can hold back the ravages of time, but we cannot escape it. Death is the price we pay for life."

"Does that mean you're going to die soon?" Matal asked. "No one else, not even Shanni, knows how to defend us against the forces we experienced."

"The problem is that I do not have enough strength remaining to me to withstand them alone. I must train you, Aurel, and others to fight in the alternate world."

"Aurel has the training and the predisposition. I am afraid I only focus on the everyday world of reality. You must find someone else."

"You are right. While you are a strong leader of the Huastecs, you can follow but you cannot lead in the alternate world. We must find one with the strength to lead."

"Who can that be?"

""I'm afraid only the Anglo has the potential."

"But how can he be trained? He does not believe the alternate world exists. He thinks we are hallucinating."

"That is the challenge, and we must solve it soon. Somehow we must bring him to believe."

Matal shook his head and fought despair. Such enormous obstacles and the Huastecs' journey had hardly begun.

Caleb led Shanni along the shadows of a canyon as the sun rose on the second day. As they passed a gully, a cool breeze brought the scent of water. Caleb turned and climbed along the dry watercourse until they rounded a bend to find a small seep surrounded by sparse desert plants. Caleb tested the water. It was brackish but safe to drink. Caleb motioned Shanni to drink, then stretched out and quenched his thirst.

"That's a gift of the gods," he observed as he carefully filled the water bag.

Shanni smiled, embarrassed, as she brushed a loose strand of hair out of her face. She was covered with trail dust, but she was never more beautiful, Caleb thought, reaching out to hold her to him for a long moment.

He released her and motioned her to stay while he moved down the gully to check their exit. He walked toward the bend as Shanni turned to prepare for travel.

Caleb neared the bend when a sudden sound warned him and he dropped to one knee, turning. He recognized the fierce visage of Chama as Chama sliced wickedly with his knife. White-hot pain flashed along Caleb's shoulder as the knife sliced along his arm. Chama swung the knife up to disembowel Caleb as he dodged and smashed a hard blow to Chama's forearm. Chama closed and they struggled, trying to gain solid footing in the sandy wash. Chama jerked back, throwing Caleb off his feet. Caleb rolled and drew his boots up as Chama leapt forward. They struggled in the blinding dust as Caleb fought to avoid a fatal thrust.

Caleb heard a sodden blow and Chama fell to back to lie motionless. Shanni stood over Chama trembling with a rifle in her hands.

"I did not know how to shoot the weapon," she explained. "So I hit him."

Caleb took the rifle from her. "We'll have to remedy that, but you did just fine."

Caleb turned to examine Chama, who was bleeding heavily. Shanni turned her head away, fighting nausea. Had she killed him? She had never hurt anyone before and now she had killed a man.

"He's alive," Caleb said. "I ought to shoot him while I have the chance. He would show us no mercy."

Shanni looked at him, shocked. "Could you kill him, lying there?"

Caleb met her gaze. "I reckon not, but we'll live to be sorry. He'll hound us and kill us if he can."

Shanni shook her head. "He'll know we spared his life. Surely he would not kill us now."

Caleb shook his head and turned to search for Chama's horse. In a short while he returned and swung Shanni up behind him. He nudged the horse down the gully and turned eastward.

Hours later, Caleb pulled up to let the horse rest. Shanni had been strangely quiet and Caleb turned around to look at her.

"I thought I had killed Chama," she said and shuddered. "All that blood after I swung the rifle. I felt horrible."

"We'd be better off if you had."

"I'm glad I did not kill him."

Caleb understood her relief. Shanni was traumatized by the fierceness of the desert where killing was a way of life. She had not yet learned that killing was necessary to survival. It was a hard lesson to learn, and it changed a person. He would protect her from learning that lesson if he could.

He felt her cling to him, her face against his back as he nudged the horse forward. They had to get out of this desert. He wanted to rescue the Huastecs and get them settled somewhere close and safe, and then he would take Shanni back to the cool meadows of the Mancos Valley. There they could be happy. That was where they belonged.

Presently Shanni took a deep breath and spoke in his ear. "I'm sorry, I lost my nerve for a moment. I am all right now."

"You're doing fine. It's a hard land."

Near sundown they topped a knoll to see a flock of sheep moving slowly in the distance. He saw a boy pointing and calling to an old man, who got up from camp and waited patiently.

"Tsiping," Caleb said as they approached, "Take us to Manuelito."

Chapter 13

The morning sun cast bright light over Manuelito's camp as Caleb and Shanni strolled in the shade of the cottonwoods lining the small river. Camp dogs cavorted with playing children in the open areas between the dwellings. The peaceful scene belied the problems still facing Manuelito and the Huastecs. Shanni was silent, reluctant to break the spell. They paused, listening to the ripple of the water over the gravel bed.

"You're quiet today," Caleb observed.

"I am worried. I fear for Tonah and the others."

"I know, but our best chance is to wait until the soldiers can go with us."

"I feel a strange dread as if my people are in grave danger."

"We must have faith that they are no worse off for the present."

He saw her expression darken. "I mean I am sure they have not been harmed. Kaibito still needs them for the mine." They sat lost in thought, watching the water flow quietly.

"What about us, Shanni? I feel the pressure of time. Soon we'll be caught up by events and pulled along. I want us to be married, now, while we have the chance."

Shanni laid her face against his shoulder. "Nothing would make me happier than to be your wife. I have dreamed of that moment, but I want it to be the ceremony of my people with Tonah and the leaders of the Huastecs joining us. I cannot marry until my people are safe. You understand, don't you?"

Caleb nodded. He understood but that did not make it easier. They could not think of their happiness while the Huastecs were in danger. He remembered the night that Tonah had rescued him and carried him all night to hide him from his enemies. He was obligated to the Huastecs. He must find a way to help them.

"But know this," Shanni continued. "I love you and want to be your wife. Know this above all else."

He reached out and held her to him. "I love you too. I just want us to be together, safe and happy."

"I pray we will not be separated again. I can bear anything if we are together."

They turned, lost in thought, and made their way back along the river to the settlement.

The quiet of the afternoon was broken by the clamor of horses as Caleb and Manuelito walked out to view the arriving cavalry. The troop was in bad shape. Several of the riders wore bandages and Caleb saw that the group was reduced to little more than a squad. The troopers must have met more trouble after Caleb had left them.

Lieutenant Porter waved a greeting and set his men to camp. Fires were started and food prepared. After a quick meal, Porter joined Manuelito and Caleb in Manuelito's lodge.

"Well, we met real trouble, as you can see," Porter said, after the usual greetings. "I think we came plumb up against Kaibito's stronghold. They fought like cats and there were a hell of a lot of them!"

"How far?" Caleb queried.

"Three days' ride due west. We were lucky to get out like we did. I sent a rider to Fort Defiance for help, but their troops were all down south."

"What do you plan to do?"

"Reckon I'll let the men and hosses rest up and then it's back to Fort Wingate. I'll recommend a full field force to march against Kaibito."

Porter bent a piercing gaze on Manuelito, who sat silently, listening.

"Manuelito, I reckon you're gonna have to choose. Kaibito's on the Navaho reservation and he's killed soldiers of the U.S. Army. We've got to track him down and you and your men will be expected to help. That's all there is to it."

Manuelito chose his words carefully when he answered. "Manuelito and his people want to live in peace. We will provide you food and shelter, and we will care for your wounded. In the treaty with your government, I was promised that if we laid aside our weapons the bluecoats would protect us. I do not agree with

Kaibito nor do I condone his acts, but I do not wish to lead my young men to their deaths against their own people."

"Reckon the army don't see it that way," Porter replied. "But you don't have to agree now. We'll rest here a mite and then we'll go on to the fort. When we return, best you be ready to ride with us."

Porter did not wait for a reply, rose, and left the lodge.

Manuelito broke the silence. "I'd like to walk. Would you go with me?"

Caleb nodded and followed Manuelito among the lodges toward the river. Children played and the women moved about the camp. Only a few white-haired men were in evidence.

As they walked along the river, Manuelito drew up to his full height and halted. He let out a deep breath, calming himself, and then spoke.

"Manuelito remembers the hot blood of war, when he led his young warriors, many men on many horses. We fought the bluecoats and sent them running away. Kaibito fought with us. He was a great warrior, very brave and fierce. None could stand before us. We celebrated our victories protecting our people and our way of life and then we returned to peace, planting our crops and raising our flocks."

"A season passed and then the bluecoats returned, but they did not fight. Instead they rode the length and breadth of the Navaho lands, and everywhere they rode they burned and lay waste the crops of the Navaho. They killed all living things. They were a scourge that brought starvation to the women and children, and despair to the hearts of the warriors.

"So they could eat, the people were forced to submit to the bluecoats at the forts. There they were treated like animals. Mothers were separated from their children and their husbands and then the people were forced to march to the harsh lands to the east. Many died. Many of those who completed the march succumbed to the white man's diseases and the rotten food. Kaibito experienced this with the people and it affected his mind. He cannot forget and he cannot forgive.

"But I remember him as a great warrior, steadfast in battle and a friend to all the Navaho. His strong arms lifted me wounded from the field of battle and bore me away to safety. Now the pony soldier asks me to choose. I must choose between the safety of my people and the life of Kaibito. Lieutenant Porter does not realize what he asks of a warrior."

Caleb nodded. He knew Manuelito could not risk further trouble with the government. The Navaho settlement was little enough. Manuelito was fighting for the survival of his people. But could he ride against Kaibito? Could he lead the enemies of his race against his own people?

Caleb could think of nothing to say. How could he lessen Manuelito's agony? Silently he gripped Manuelito's arm and turned away.

Manuelito sagged as if a great breath had gone out of him. He looked old and tired as he led the way back to the camp.

Manuelito turned to Caleb before entering his lodge. "Thank you for understanding. I see why the Huastec princess has given you her heart. Only Manuelito can decide the course to take and all the choices are filled with pain."

Caleb walked away, lost in thought. His steps carried him to the soldiers' camp. Porter was holding a cup of coffee and acknowledged Caleb's presence with a nod. Porter filled another cup and passed it as Caleb sat down by the fire.

"Reckon you think I'm a son-of-a-bitch, leanin' on Manuelito like that," Porter said.

"To be honest, I don't know what to think anymore," Caleb answered.

Porter seemed preoccupied, musing to himself. "You see, I left men stretched out back there, blackening in the blazin' sun. Good men, that's followed me into battle many a time. Kaibito's still walking around, waitin' to dish out more of the same. I reckon the time's come to end it, and I will use every means at my disposal to get it done!"

Caleb understood where Porter was coming from. A career soldier led a hard life with a bullet likely to end it. All that made sense in Porter's world was to strike at his enemies until he was too old, or until he himself was stretched out upon some strange battlefield.

"You may not know what you're asking of Manuelito. Kaibito was one of his trusted men, a warrior and a friend. To Manuelito, riding against Kaibito is like riding against his own family."

Porter looked up at Caleb and thought a moment.

"No offense, Stone, but you're a strange bird. You seem to take the Indian's side in this. Them's white men stretched out back there. Can you forget that?"

"No, I reckon I can't. It's just that I can see Manuelito's quandary."

"Wal, I'm not given to philosophy. I'm just trying to live up to what the good ol' U.S. of A. expects of me. It may be a hard choice, but Manuelito's got to go along. He'll see it and he'll do it."

Porter sat sipping his coffee and gazing into the fire. He avoided Caleb's eyes.

Caleb pondered for long moments, trying to decide if he should confide in Porter. "Porter, I reckon I can trust you and I sure need your help. Kaibito's got a band of Indians called the 'Huastecs' as his prisoners."

"Never heard of any such."

"You wouldn't have. They've been hidden away up in the mountains of the Colorados. They're trying to find their way south to their people. The Indian woman I brought back with me is Huastec and part Spanish. I plan to marry her, but first I aim to help rescue the Huastecs."

"Wal, I can't promise anything. My orders are to get Kaibito and his followers and take 'em in. Reckon that includes all the Indians in his camp."

"I want to ride with you when you go for Kaibito. We must find a way to get the Huastecs out before Kaibito turns on them."

"That'll be a tall order, because Kaibito will likely fight to the death if he's cornered. He's a bad one. If he has to cut and run, prisoners will be in his way. He'll probably kill them all."

Caleb nodded. He'd considered that possibility and knew he must find a way to rescue the Huastecs before Porter and his soldiers rode Kaibito to ground.

The next morning, Porter and his soldiers left for the fort. Manuelito remained silent and kept to his lodge. Caleb was thoughtful and Shanni picked up his change in mood. They spent much of the day together, silently aware of the certainty that this respite would end and fate might again separate them.

As the time passed, a plan took form in Caleb's mind. He knew he could not share his plan with Shanni, for she could not help and did not need more to worry about. Coldness gripped his heart knowing he must leave her to return, alone, to Kaibito's camp.

Caleb confided in Manuelito who did not attempt to dissuade him. Manuelito understood what had to be done. He provided Caleb a fine horse and provisions, and then gripped his hand silently as Caleb prepared to ride out in the darkness.

SUTTON'S SALOON WAS a low, log structure located a few hundred yards from the entrance to Fort Defiance. A disreputable place, it hugged the security of the fort while providing a watering hole for transients and the freighter traffic into the fort.

Trooper Smith stopped on his way out of the fort to have a drink and cool his anger. His message from Porter to the commander had not been well received. There was Indian trouble down south and the commander could spare no troops to support Porter. Porter would have to make do for himself.

The harsh liquor settled his nerves and Smith began to relax, becoming aware of his surroundings. A couple of riders were nursing drinks further down the bar and Smith felt like company.

"Evenin', boys," he opened, lifting his glass.

The men nodded, lifting their glasses in a return salute. Smith moved down and engaged the men in conversation, sharing news. The drink made Smith expansive and he forgot caution as he asked questions.

"What brings you to these parts?"

Wilson glanced at Ralph, but answered genially.

"Looking for a man by the name of Caleb Stone. You seen or heard tell of him?"

Smith paused, cautious. Asking after a man could be a threat; answering wrong could get a man shot. Wilson read the indecision and waited.

"It can be positively unhealthy to speak out of turn about a man," Smith answered. "Especially if the man is hunted."

"Nothing like that," Wilson smiled. "We're neighbors. Thought he'd like to know he has a new son to welcome him home when he gets back, is all. We're headed south. He's been away and doubt he's heard."

"Well, now," Smith relaxed. "That's good news, and no offense meant. Fact is, I did see him. He rode with us hunting the Navaho renegade Kaibito. I thought it was curious that he seemed to have business with Kaibito. Not that it would do him any good. Likely Kaibito will come back laid over a saddle."

Smith remembered he had a long ride to Fort Wingate and finished his drink. Taking his leave, he walked out of the low-ceilinged room.

Wilson pondered, sipping his drink. "It's a small world, ain't it? Here we've been selling rifles to Kaibito and he's got something we want. I guess we better drift over to Lee's Ferry and look him up."

Chapter 14

Shanni walked alone among the cottonwoods that lined the river. She gazed unseeing with her heart bursting. She had a foreboding that something terrible was about to happen to Caleb. She and Caleb had walked this very path and he had been strangely preoccupied. The next day, when Manuelito delivered his message, she found out that Caleb was gone.

Caleb was returning to attempt to rescue the Huastecs and Shanni blamed herself. By her words, she had inadvertently placed the burden for the Huastecs' fate upon him. She realized she had sent him into almost certain death. Why had she not seen more clearly? By marrying him she could devote her life to being happy and making him happy. By focusing on her duty to her people she stood to lose everything. How had she become so blind? What had happened to her Gift to see dimly into the future and avoid danger?

Self-doubt racked Shanni, alone in her anguish. Now she could do nothing but wait, prisoner to the events she had set in motion.

She sat down in the glade, overcome by her emotions. Silent tears streamed down her face.

A soft rustle startled her and she looked up to see Manuelito standing nearby, his eyes soft.

"I am sorry to intrude, little princess, but I was worried about you. Caleb asked me to look to your care. He said you should not blame yourself for he had no other choice."

"I know," Shanni gasped. "I am the one who created that choice!"

"You do not understand. It was not your words that created the choice."

"What, then?"

"He did not want me to add to your worry, but I know that no anguish compares to that directed at oneself."

"Thank you, Manuelito. You are being kind, but I must face myself. I fear my words sent Caleb to his death for my sake."

Manuelito gazed across the placid stream, thinking. Nearby a bird called and Shanni became aware of the low murmur of the water. Finally Manuelito turned to her, gripping her by the shoulders.

"He did not go because of your words. He went because of the words of the pony soldier Porter."

Shanni felt a sense of foreboding wash over her, replacing the anguish. She read the truth in Manuelito's words and feared what he was about to reveal.

"Porter told Caleb he would return with a large force and he would march against Kaibito until Kaibito was captured or killed. Porter said that when Kaibito is forced to flee, he will likely kill all the prisoners."

Shanni felt an icy coldness envelop her. Of course she had known of the possibility, but she thought they had time. There had been no indication that Kaibito planned to leave his camp. But now that Porter was pushing forward, time was running out. She thought of Tonah. He would stay with his people to the last and share their fate. Matal, strong and full of the fire of youth, would fight, but without weapons he would perish.

Manuelito led her back to the village. As she entered her quarters, Manuelito gazed after her, his brow creased with worry. Sometimes it was more terrible to wait than to act, even against the odds.

He returned to his lodge and sat silently before the fire, impervious to the passing hours.

Mid-morning of the next day a young rider came in from the outlying flocks. He rode directly to Manuelito's lodge to announce the return of the bluecoats. Excitement filled the air as a bustle of activity sent puffs of dust through the compound.

Manuelito walked outside and sat down to await the arrival of the soldiers. He breathed deeply, savoring the morning air. He took pleasure in the peaceful scene before him. His people lived without fear after many years of deprivation. Whatever his failures, he had lived to see his people at peace, and his heart was full.

A child ran by and stopped to romp on his knee. Manuelito cuffed him gently and the boy laughed. Manuelito's vision dimmed for a moment and he knew what he must do. The decision made, he felt the burden lift from his shoulders and he drew strength from strong, deep breaths. He rose to his full height and turned into his dwelling. When he emerged, he wore the utilitarian garments of the Navaho warrior. He sent word by an aide and soon his call to arms was transmitted to the young men of the camp.

Shanni approached as he stood waiting. "May I talk with you?"

"Of course. You do not need permission to speak with me!"

"I'm sorry, but you look so fierce in your battle clothes. I came to thank you for telling me the reason for Caleb's leaving. It helps to know. But there's more. Caleb told me of Porter's ultimatum to you. Do you intend to ride with him against Kaibito?"

"Yes. I will ride with the soldiers against Kaibito."

"You know that if Kaibito escapes, he will seek revenge against you and your people."

"Yes. My people die if I do not go and my people die if Kaibito lives. Therefore I must go and I must see that Kaibito does not live. That is my gift to my people."

Shanni was stunned. Gentle Manuelito had spoken with authority. She felt the strength of conviction within him. He was a formidable war chief who had chosen peace. Now he would do what he had to do. She nodded and turned away. What could she say? She stood by watching as Manuelito led the young men away to join the soldiers.

She was left alone with the activities of the camp and the torment of her thoughts. Foreboding filled her and her hands trembled as she worked at her duties. Her mind was far away. Had Caleb confided in her, she would have insisted on going with him and sharing his fate, and she realized that was why he had not told her. Could she bear to be left alive if Caleb was killed and the Huastecs perished?

Near dusk she wandered again to the small glade near the river, seeking peace. She was lost in her thoughts when a hard hand clasped her mouth, stifling her scream. Strong arms lifted her and dragged her into the willows and pushed her to the ground. She recognized the fierce visage of Chama in the dim light.

Chapter 15

The late evening sun cast long shadows across the arroyos as Caleb climbed the deep gully. He was a gray apparition covered with dust leading a heavily laden packhorse in the vast emptiness. His eyes roved restlessly scanning the surrounding terrain. He saw and approached a hollow in the wall of the gully and poked his rifle inside. He expected the whirr of rattles but the hollow was empty. He unloaded rifles and ammunition from the packhorse. After hiding them in the shallow cave, he erased his tracks and signs of his passage.

Satisfied, he remounted and continued past the gully into a narrow canyon that led away to the northwest. Dusk was falling as he reached the entrance to the park leading to Kaibito's camp.

Caleb dismounted and returned to the packhorse. He removed wood he had brought for a fire and placed it in the soft sand. He walked forward several steps and stacked his rifle and revolver in plain view. He returned to the wood and placed stones for a small fire. He lit the wood and sat cross-legged to wait in the light from the flames.

Hours had passed when a voice broke the stillness.

"Do not move or it is your life."

"I have no intention of moving," Caleb answered. "I wait to see Kaibito."

"Kaibito does not welcome strangers."

"I am no stranger. I am Caleb Stone. Kaibito will see me and hear the message I bring from Manuelito."

"What is the message?"

"I will give it only to Kaibito."

"Then you die where you sit!"

"And you will die when Kaibito finds out what you did."

A long silence passed.

"Get up and walk forward. Do not go near the guns. I have a rifle and I will shoot you if you try anything."

Caleb heard the man gathering the reins of the horse and picking up his guns as he walked in the direction of Kaibito's camp. As they walked, the cool desert wind moved around them, whipping sand in thin sheets across the valley floor. A pale moon illuminated their path and Caleb recognized the Chaco ruins on the valley floor.

An hour's walk brought them to the entrance to Kaibito's camp. Caleb's captor answered a sharp challenge and they paused. Moments later, two guards arrived and Caleb heard the three men talking. He was nudged forward with the rifle and soon reached Kaibito's camp. There was no sign of the Huastecs. The camp was heavily guarded. He would have little hope of escape if his plan did not work.

He saw silent riders seated around the campfire.

"I would speak with Kaibito," Caleb demanded. "Take me to him."

"He is not here. You will wait until he returns."

Caleb's arms and legs were bound and he was dropped in the shadows. An armed guard sat nearby watching him. The hours passed slowly as Caleb dozed. The next morning Caleb's hands were untied and he was given food and water. The camp was quiet with an attitude of waiting. Caleb saw a familiar form exit from one of the dwellings and recognized Chama. Chama turned and their eyes met. Chama smiled evilly and turned away. Chama will do the honors, Caleb thought, if Kaibito gives the order to kill me.

Night had fallen when the muffled sounds of hooves broke the stillness. Kaibito and his riders appeared out of the gloom and set about dismounting and unloading the horses. They turned to the campfire and began eating in silence. After eating, Kaibito gathered the men around him to converse quietly. One of the riders left the group and moved toward Caleb. The rider hauled him to his feet and removed the bindings from his feet. A rifle barrel prodded him on numb feet to the light of the fire.

Kaibito eyed him coldly. "So you bring a message from Manuelito? What is it?"

"Manuelito fears for Kaibito. Many soldiers are coming. Kaibito and those who follow him will be killed. Manuelito does not forget his brother. If you will give yourself up into his care, he will negotiate your surrender to the soldiers so that you will not be harmed."

"Why does he send word by a white man? Manuelito is welcome in my camp."

"He must stay and look to the welfare of his people. Your actions are endangering all the Navaho."

"Bah! Manuelito has become an old woman. He has forgotten the time of sorrows, but I do not forget. And I do not forgive! Many more soldiers will die at my hand in payment for the sufferings of the Navaho."

"If you will not take Manuelito's offer, allow me to lead the Huastecs away. They have done you no harm and will only be in your way. That is the reason I came."

"Why do you care what happens to the Huastecs?"

"I owe my life to the old one, Tonah. He saved me from my enemies. I promised to guide him and his people to their home to the south."

"I will think about it," Kaibito answered with a dismissive wave of his hand. The guard prodded Caleb back to his seat in the shadows and re-tied his feet. Caleb shifted, trying to get comfortable as Kaibito walked toward the low buildings.

Caleb had dozed when the approach of soft steps awakened him.

Chama's face appeared dimly in the light of the campfire.

"Kaibito sends you a message. I told Kaibito how I watched Manuelito leave his camp riding with the soldiers. Kaibito says that Manuelito is no longer his brother, and no longer your protector. Tomorrow I will set you free to wander forever in the spirit world. Kaibito has spoken!"

Chama chuckled and glided away.

The fire burned low as the camp settled into sleep, but Caleb's mind was working feverishly. His plan had failed because of Chama. He should have finished him back there on the desert. Somehow Chama had managed to get close enough to the soldiers to see Manuelito, and that meant Manuelito had chosen to help the soldiers. His gamble had failed and he would share the fate of the Huastecs. At least Shanni was safe!

Chapter 16

Kaibito was deep in thought as he weighed action for the next few days. All his plans were nearing fruition. His raids had gained him fame with the renegades along the border and a large force was moving to join him. He knew the soldiers were riding from Fort Wingate. When they attacked, he could hold them off from the camp while his new force caught the soldiers in a pincers, cutting off their escape. His men would kill them all and capture many horses, rifles and ammunition. Kaibito smiled at the thought. He would no longer be dependent upon trade with the white-eyes at Lee's Ferry.

Kaibito knew this was a critical juncture. He was in a position to strike a telling blow at the U.S. government. His fame would grow and with it the number of warriors eager to join him in a war of liberation. He would have his revenge with the deaths of scores of soldiers for each Navaho who had died. The white-eyes would be forced to sue for peace on Kaibito's terms and he would become the savior of the Navaho nation. Manuelito would see the folly of his ways in catering to the white-eyes.

Manuelito was acting strange lately. Why had he provided protection to Caleb Stone? Stone had escaped once and must know it was certain death to return. Why would a white man risk his life to rescue the Huastecs? None of this made any sense and he had no time for distractions. He must focus on annihilating the soldiers when they appeared.

"It was a good day's work, my friend," he said to Chama who lounged near the campfire. "And tomorrow you shall have your reward."

Chama smiled. He was in high favor with Kaibito since he'd spied on Manuelito and brought news of his actions. Finding and returning the slave girl had been a fortunate accident that had salved Kaibito's displeasure at her escape. Maybe when he tired of her he would pass her around. She was young; she would last awhile.

Kaibito's thoughts turned to Shanni. Maybe he would go to her and see if she'd lost that arrogant attitude now that she saw his power over her and all of the Huastecs.

He lifted the bottle of tequila he'd brought from Mexico and took a long drink. He watched Chama walk over to Stone in the shadows and grinned. Chama would tell him what to expect. Chama knew how to draw the last bit of suffering out of a man. Stone would not sleep tonight knowing what he faced tomorrow.

Shanni had been numb with fatigue when the horse stopped and Chama pulled her from the saddle. He had dragged her to Kaibito's dwelling and left her to huddle miserably on her old bed. She was helpless and back where she had started. Why had things gone so wrong for the Huastecs?

She eased up to gaze out the window toward the campfires. A commotion caught her eyes and she was shocked to recognize Caleb being dragged before Kaibito. So he was also a captive. Her heart sank. His mission had failed. Even if the soldiers came, the Huastecs could look forward only to death, not rescue.

Anger overcame her and for the first time in her life she knew hatred. This was Chama's fault. Chama was the spoiler, and Caleb would have killed him but for her. Now Caleb's life and all their lives would be forfeit. How had she been so naïve? Now she understood how Caleb had learned to kill.

With hatred came a terrible resolve. She would do what she had to do. She returned to the pallet and settled down to plan.

Moments later she heard noise outside and heard Kaibito approaching. He appeared in the doorway and paused, smiling.

"We are back to where we began. Have you learned manners yet?"

"What do you intend to do with Caleb Stone?"

"Oh, so you know him. What do you care what happens to him?"

"He is a friend of my people."

"Well, your people's friend will taste death at the hands of Chama tomorrow. He's caused us enough trouble."

"He is only here because he tried to help us. He does not deserve to die."

"He is a white-eye. That is enough."

Shanni steadied herself to do what she must do.

"You told me once you would not have me until I came begging to you. Do you remember?"

"I remember."

Kaibito was smiling again. She was coming around. Women always did. They could not resist his power.

"Very well. I am coming to you now."

Shanni approached him and slid her arms around his neck.

"I will do anything you want if you free Caleb Stone."

Shanni's eyes smoldered and Kaibito licked his lips. This was what he wanted but why was she suddenly so willing? The truth hit him and he staggered back.

"You love the white-eye! That is why you have come to me!"

"I've offered you a fair trade, what you want for what I want."

Madness crept into Kaibito's eyes as he burst out, stuttering with strong emotion.

"You, an Indian, care for a white-eye, the murderers of our people! You are worse than the bought women of the towns. You are a traitor to our people..."

Kaibito stopped and regained control with an effort. He spoke coldly.

"I would not defile myself with you."

He moved to go and stopped in the doorway, turning back to her.

"I will see to it that you watch Stone die."

Shanni sank back in despair. She had offered everything to save Caleb and she had failed.

Chapter 17

It was late at night, but Caleb had not slept. He strained to loosen his bonds but they only became tighter, cutting off circulation and causing constant pain. The guard remained nearby so that Caleb could not move about.

A shadow flickered near the pool of water. Caleb blinked. Maybe his tired eyes were playing tricks on him. A hand pressed firmly across his mouth and then the pressure lessened and the hand moved away. Caleb had heard nothing but he understood the warning to remain silent.

His eyes returned to the guard sitting against a pile of gear. The guard's head flew back and Caleb heard a low, gurgling sound. The guard's head tilted forward and hung loosely on his chest. Caleb felt a knife working through his bonds and his hands fell free. He rolled back into the shadows and climbed to his knees.

"Follow me," Manuelito's voice came to him in a low whisper.

They crawled away from camp and Manuelito spoke hurriedly.

"We must get the Huastecs out right away. The soldiers plan to attack at dawn!"

"We'll need guns. I have rifles hidden..."

"No time," Manuelito cut in. "You get the Huastecs moving while I get the rifles. I'll meet you at the head of the canyon."

Caleb described the hiding place of the rifles as Manuelito slid a revolver and knife into his hands and then disappeared into the shadows.

Caleb moved to the area of the pool near the canyon wall where he had last seen the Huastecs sleeping in the shadows. No one was there. He looked around in desperation. What had happened to them? He hugged the shadows and continued up the canyon. He entered the side canyon that contained the silver mine and saw the silent shapes of the Huastec men sprawled in sleep near the entrance to the mine.

Kaibito must have moved them closer so he could herd them inside and dynamite the opening if he were attacked.

Tonah's breathing was labored as Caleb approached to shake him awake. It seemed to Caleb that Tonah took an unusually long time to rouse and become aware of his surroundings.

Finally, Tonah's mind cleared and he recognized Caleb.

"The work has robbed our bodies of their strength," Tonah said. "And we have enemies to fight in the world of energy."

"No time to talk. We must go now, the soldiers attack at dawn. Kaibito will kill us all if we're still here." Caleb moved away to awake the others.

Tonah started to rise when the clink of chains reminded him of the leg irons. He picked them up and followed Caleb to awaken the others. Soon all the Huastec men were awake and moving in the shadows past the campfire where Kaibito's men slept.

A horse snorted, sounding an alarm, and a sleeping rider leapt up, revolver in hand. Caleb's shot felled him in his tracks, but it was a free-for-all now. Forsaking silence, the Huastec men gathered up their chains and mounted the horses, riding through the camp to cover the escape of the women and children down the canyon. Manuelito met them at the mouth of the canyon and distributed rifles to the men as the women and children continued their escape across the park.

"Shoot your chains free," Caleb commanded, "And form a line of defense. We must stay and cover the others' escape."

He heard hoof beats approaching down the canyon. Kaibito's men were awake and in pursuit. Caleb turned and saw that the Huastecs were running across the plain toward the cliff dwelling, but they were not far enough. If Kaibito's men got past, the Huastecs would be slaughtered!

Caleb fired and the men laid down a withering fire up the canyon as the riders approached. Screams and the sound of horses falling told Caleb the bullets had found targets. The crash of gravel signaled the remaining riders dismounting, followed by a hail of bullets as they returned fire.

They had lost the element of surprise, Caleb thought, and Kaibito's men were seasoned fighters. The inexperienced

Huastecs were in a desperate position. Manuelito realized the danger and led the men to take up positions for crossfire on the canyon exit. Kaibito's men were trapped for the present, but they could move more freely on foot. Kaibito's men took positions and began firing. Their bullets reached the Huastecs with devastating effect.

"We've got to fall back in waves," Caleb shouted. "Every other man fall back a hundred paces the fire over the others as they retreat. Continue until we reach the cliffs."

They began moving across the open valley. They gained a temporary advantage as Kaibito's men moved from cover and attempted to follow. The advantage would shift, Caleb realized, when they reached the face of the cliff. They would be picked off if they tried to climb to the cliff dwellings.

A new line of fire opened up from the southwest, wreaking havoc on Kaibito's advance fighters and forcing the others back into the canyon. The break permitted Caleb and the others to sprint for the cliffs in relative safety. They could hear the battle raging behind them, but the attack was broken and they were out of range. They climbed the rock face to the plaza of the cliff dwellings and took stock. Some were wounded but everyone was accounted for. They were safe for the present.

"I believe you pulled it off, Manuelito," Caleb said. "What's going on down there?"

"The soldiers had planned to attack at dawn. I talked Porter into letting me try to get everyone out. That's his men lending a hand now."

"We're safe for now but we can't stay here. Let's hope Porter and his men can finish the job."

JORGE TUPAC AWAKENED, weak and hungry. He accepted food from Ramon's wife with gratitude and made his way outside to sit in the doorway. He ate and drank slowly, watching the long shadows of the afternoon sun move across the landscape. The food refreshed him, giving him strength, and he went to the water basin to clean up. He washed slowly, taking his time to gain control of the anger that filled him. He had resumed his normal persona and was calm by the time Ramon returned from the fields.

"Jorge, it is good to see you awake. We feared for you. Did you fall into the fire?"

"You will not believe this, Ramon. Late in the afternoon, a storm blew in and I was nearly killed by the lightning that struck a nearby tree!"

"A storm is rare in these mountains, and to be struck by lightning! Surely the gods protected you or you would be dead!"

Jorge grinned foolishly. "I was unwise to stay out in the open and ignore the danger."

"Stay with us for a few days and regain your strength."

"Thank you for the offer, but I must be on my way. I have much to attend to."

Jorge loaded his few possessions and waved goodbye, leading the burro toward the south. Ramon shook his head as he watched Jorge depart. Jorge had neither land nor family, and few possessions. What business could the old man have that was so urgent? Who could understand the ways of Jorge?

Chapter 18

Lieutenant Porter was a seasoned Indian fighter. He knew he could not move a large troop across country without Kaibito becoming aware of it. Never the less, he had traveled with the troop at night in the hope he could catch Kaibito off guard. He had tipped his hand by assisting the Huastecs, but so be it. He had a freer hand with them out of Kaibito's camp.

As dawn broke, he prepared to tighten the noose. He placed some of his men on the canyon rim, while the main part of his troop dug in at the entrance to Kaibito's camp. The cliff dwellings were across the valley to the north. He set up a gun emplacement with a 3-inch howitzer. Using it as cover, they could charge the canyon and Kaibito's camp.

The first howitzer round shattered rock over the heads of Kaibito's advance guard. The troops on the canyon rim opened fire, driving Kaibito's men from their positions to retreat in disarray up the canyon. Additional rounds followed them up the canyon, bursting among the horses and causing a near rout. Porter pushed his advantage, marching in force up the canyon. Kaibito and his men abandoned the dwellings and retreated up the canyon containing the silver mine. Caleb and Manuelito secured provisions and ammunition from the troops at the gun emplacement and hurried back to protect the Huastecs. The canyon narrowed as Porter and his men advanced and resistance stiffened. Kaibito's men were dug in as the battle settled into a duel with rifles. The day dragged, with Porter unable to advance and Kaibito unwilling to retreat further.

Caleb could see the battle from his perch on the plaza of the cliff dwelling. Toward dusk, he saw heavily armed riders enter the valley, hugging the cliffs to the south. As they neared the entrance to the canyon, they dismounted and threw up earthworks, blocking Porter's retreat. Leaving a rear-guard, the riders advanced up the canyon. Caleb saw why Kaibito had played a waiting game. He had expected reinforcements, and now Porter's strategy had taken a turn for the worse.

A shell burst back down the canyon, followed by the heavy boom of the howitzer.

Caleb turned to Tonah and Matal. "Porter has discovered the attackers on his flank and realizes he's trapped."

"We must do something," Matal said. "We cannot allow our rescuers to be overcome."

Caleb nodded agreement, but what was to be done? They would be sitting ducks on foot crossing the valley.

"We still have the element of surprise," he said, "But what we do must work the first time." Caleb hurried to familiarize the young men of the Huastecs with the rifles and ammunition as they waited for nightfall.

At dusk a shadow moved along the canyon wall and climbed the steps leading to the cliff dwellings.

"Hold your fire," Caleb cautioned. "It's Manuelito returning."

Manuelito reached the plaza and stopped to catch his breath. He'd had a difficult time getting past the attackers.

"What's Porter's situation?" Caleb asked.

"Not desperate yet, but he is trapped. Neither of Kaibito's groups can reach him until he runs low on ammunition, but he is vulnerable to a coordinated attack. When Kaibito and his men are willing to pay the price, they'll rush Porter. Porter wants out before that happens. You and the Huastecs are now key to the battle."

"He wants us to open up behind this bunch and distract them while he breaks out, I reckon."

"Exactly. A diversion at the right time will make the difference."

Caleb thought a moment. Despite the Huastec's inexperience in battle, they had to do it. Without Porter's protection, the Huastecs would be at the mercy of Kaibito and his men. If Kaibito ran free, there would be a bloodbath.

"When?"

"At first light."

Caleb looked at Tonah and Matal. It was up to them to speak for their men. They nodded, and Caleb turned to Manuelito.

"Tell Porter we'll be there."

"One thing," Caleb added as Manuelito turned to go down the cliff face. "Remind Porter that we'll be defenseless on foot once Kaibito's rear guard turns on us. They'll ride us down like dogs. Tell Porter to come roaring with his howitzer blazing. If he fails, we're done."

Manuelito nodded. He knew the risk, and he understood what Caleb could not say. The Huastecs were brave but they were not seasoned fighters. They would only be effective a short time. After the initial surprise, Kaibito's men would turn and overwhelm them if Porter did not quickly close behind them. It would be close.

Manuelito disappeared down the stone steps as Caleb and the Huastecs completed their preparations and tried to rest. Two hours before dawn they would start across the valley.

The full moon dipped behind a peak to the west, casting the valley floor in shadow as Caleb and the small band of eight Huastecs moved out. They were nine rifles against a seasoned band of a dozen or more, but it would have to do. Caleb turned his full attention to the task at hand. They must get close to the enemy and dig in before dawn without being discovered. There was scant cover as they neared the enemy breastworks. They lay down prone, taking advantage of slight depressions in the ground and half-buried rocks, and waited for dawn. As the light increased, they saw the attackers were already up, drinking coffee and preparing for the day's battle. Several men left the camp to relieve the men on guard at the canyon entrance.

Now is as good a time as any to start the fireworks, Caleb thought, his mouth dry. He glanced at Matal, who was pale, and saw his jaw muscles twitch. He was scared, Caleb knew, but he was game. They'd all do their best.

Caleb nodded, giving the signal to fire. The rifles roared, and bodies twisted around the campfire as bullets found their marks. Five of the enemies were down as others ran, confused, trying to mount a defense. The Huastecs levered new rounds into their carbines and fired again. The running figures dropped to the ground and returned fire, burning the ground near the Huastecs as they got the range. Enemy riders at the breastworks came running back to reinforce their companions against the new threat.

One of the Huastecs dropped his rifle, a red blotch covering his face as his head pitched forward. The way they were forced to lie, facing head-on, a hit was almost certainly fatal. Bullets were coming hard and fast, making it difficult to look up long enough to fire. They'd all be dead soon, Caleb knew, if Porter didn't get through.

He heard the roar of the howitzer as the breastworks exploded in flying dust and rock. The next shell advanced, hitting the enemy campfire and scattering hot coals in a wide radius onto the enemy fighters. Howls of anguish followed as fighters, slapping at the hot coals, twisted into view.

Caleb and the remaining Huastecs levered shots at the riders, pinning them down as Porter's cavalry approached riding hard to pour withering fire into the enemy flanks.

Resistance broke as some of the riders charged for their horses in an attempt to get away from the carnage. Porter's men bore down on the survivors and the battle was over in minutes. The few remaining enemy riders dropped their weapons and raised their hands in defeat.

Porter rode over to the Huastecs and shouted hurriedly, "We did it, thanks to all of you. You gave us the edge we needed. Now for the fox himself!"

He wheeled his horse to lead the charge back up the canyon.

Caleb stood up and turned to the Huastecs. Matal looked at him, blinking back silent tears. Five of the Huastecs, hardly more than boys, had gotten their battle seasoning and paid with their lives. Silently Caleb helped the others gather up the bodies and begin the long walk across the valley.

Chapter 19

Flushed with the heat of battle, Porter led his men in a charge up the canyon. He met his advance guard returning and pulled to a halt. The scout named Druthers brought him news.

"Damnedest thing I ever saw, Lieutenant. They had us dead to rights and we were all set to hightail it when they pulled back. We didn't dare follow with only a few of us and your orders not to engage them."

"You did right. How long ago did they retreat?"

"Half hour, at the outside."

Porter signaled his men to advance. "Forward at a walk. Two outriders a thousand yards ahead."

The troop moved out, rifles ready. Tension lined the faces of the troopers. Kaibito's move could be a trap. Porter felt the perspiration running down his neck. You never got used to it, he thought, listening for the bullet that could kill you.

They had neared the mouth of the canyon when the first explosion rent the stillness. The earth shook and a huge cloud of dust spewed into the air. Porter and the men took cover but soon realized the explosion was not meant for them. They remounted and rode into the park where Kaibito's camp and dwellings stood empty. The explosion had come from the smaller canyon farther up. A second blast crashed down the canyon. Porter had given the signal to advance when Manuelito appeared on foot.

"What gives?" Porter asked. He was worried by the narrow passage they faced if they advanced further.

"Kaibito is gone. It is all clear now."

"Gone!" Porter was incredulous. "Just when we had brought him to his knees? How'n hell did he do it?"

"Come, I will show you."

Manuelito led off at a trot with Porter and the troop following. They reached a small glade where overturned vats and burned-out fires marked the entrance to the silver mine. The slope containing the mineshaft had been dynamited leaving only tons of broken talus. Farther up, as the draw dead-ended in a box canyon, Kaibito had blown open an exit, giving him and his men access to an adjoining canyon. Porter started to follow when a narrow turn revealed a fresh rockslide blocking his advance. Kaibito had made his exit and closed the door behind him with the second blast. Porter swore under his breath. It would take a full day to go back out of the canyon and pick up Kaibito's trail, but there was no other way now that the exit was blocked.

Porter led the troop back down the canyon and began pulling the command together. He had been wounded but overall they had gotten off lightly considering the trap by Kaibito's reinforcements. His men began bringing in the bodies of Kaibito's men. Kaibito had been dealt a serious blow, but quick follow-up was needed to finish him.

The men gathered around Porter to discuss the next move.

"Where do you think he is off to, Manuelito?" Manuelito had earned Porter's respect. He no longer called him "Chief".

"I think he will go into the badlands to the west. There he will rest and let his men recover. He will make a trip to Mexico to rearm and then I think he will return."

Porter pondered a moment. "I think you're right which means we should press him and not give him a chance to recover. Trouble is, I've got men wounded and out of action. I can't put a full force on his trail without returning to the fort for reinforcements. That would cost us several days."

"Too long," Manuelito replied. "The trail would blow away. We would never find him."

"What do you think, Caleb?"

"We have to stay after him, but I have an obligation to look to the Huastecs' welfare. They can't stay here and will need help getting back to civilization, such as it is. Plus we have five men to bury."

"Yes, and it's too bad." There was genuine regret in Porter's voice. "Those were brave lads that died doing a man's job. They deserved better."

Caleb nodded, recognizing Porter's tribute. You looked at a man differently when you got to know him.

"Well, I hate to do it but I reckon I've got to split the force. Manuelito's men estimate there are not more than a score of fighting men left in Kaibito's band. I'll pick up the able-bodied of my troop and leave a squad to escort the wounded back to the fort. The Huastecs can go along with them."

"Won't do," Caleb objected. "Like as not your commander will arrest them and put them on a reservation."

Porter thought a moment. "True enough, but what's the alternative? They can't stay here."

Manuelito spoke up. "They can stay at our camp. They'll be safe there and cared for until they're able to resume their journey."

Porter raised his eyebrows quizzically to Caleb.

"Makes sense," Caleb answered, "And I appreciate the offer. That will solve their problem for the present and free us to carry on after Kaibito. Now I have to go help the Huastecs bury their dead."

"One more thing," Manuelito spoke quietly, looking at Caleb. "It grieves me to tell you this. One of my men watched Kaibito's retreat and saw the little princess as Kaibito's captive."

Hatred flashed through Caleb. How could it have happened? Shanni had been safe at Manuelito's camp. Then he thought of Chama. Only Chama had ridden east and he had gloated at Caleb that night at the campfire. He should've killed Chama when he had the chance. Before he had wanted only to rescue the Huastecs, but now he wanted more. He wanted to move, to hound Kaibito and Chama until they and their renegades were dead.

"I'm going to bury the dead," he spoke grimly. "I'll be ready to ride with you at daybreak."

Night had fallen when Caleb and the burial detail returned to the cliff dwellings. Tonah had not attended and Caleb was worried. He asked Matal about Tonah, but Matal was noncommittal stating only that Tonah was not feeling well.

At Caleb's insistence, Matal led him across the plaza to a room in the stone apartments. Tonah was seated on a blanket, and Caleb was struck at how old and frail Tonah appeared in the light of the small fire. Tonah had aged visibly, his white hair hanging in wisps about his gaunt face. The aura of energy and vitality that had surrounded him in the past was missing. Caleb felt apprehension as he realized they could not afford to lose Tonah, too much depended on his wisdom.

"I'm pleased you came," Tonah opened. "We have much to discuss."

"You don't look well. Is there something I can get you?"

"I need no medicine. I need to call back the vitality of youth, but that is beyond reach."

"Shanni told me that you can call up energy and bend it to your needs. That is how you saved my life."

"The human body must have a certain level of energy in order to manipulate the primordial energy. I have used both to prolong my years, but there is a limit. A battle has been joined in an alternative world in which evil men seek to destroy us. I was weakened in the initial skirmish. Now that we have discovered them, they will bring greater power to bear upon us."

Caleb shook his head. The old man was rambling, talking out of his head.

"You are a fighter. You must help." Tonah continued.

"I intend to. I leave with Porter tomorrow. Kaibito has Shanni and I won't rest until I hunt him down."

"I know, but then you must help me defeat the enemies who are more powerful than Kaibito."

"I understand the enemies that I can see. I know how to use weapons to defeat them. Failure means death."

"You do not believe we have enemies in the spirit world?"

"I respect your wisdom and I am grateful to you for saving my life, but I cannot believe in a spirit world. There is only one reality for me, guns and knives against Kaibito. Perhaps Aurel or Matal can help."

"I tried, and they were willing. Their vitality saved us, but they are too young. They do not yet have the strength of will to prevail. It is your strength of intent that makes you our best hope."

Caleb did not want to argue. Tonah was weak. He needed to rest. But Tonah would not let it go.

"It is more difficult to prevail in the spirit world if one does not believe."

"Let's let it lay for now. I don't want to offend you, but I don't want to mislead you either. This talk of spirit worlds disturbs me. It sounds like witchcraft. My people do not believe in such things."

"None of us chooses the call, but we must heed it. Like you, I once resisted the irresistible. Go now. Go after Shanni. After you rescue her, we must work swiftly. I have much to teach you in the short time remaining to me."

Caleb shook his head in dismay. Tonah was gravely ill and hallucinating. He had to get Tonah to people who could help him.

"Manuelito has agreed to give the Huastecs refuge until this is over. You will all travel with Porter's troop until you reach Manuelito's camp. You'll be safe there. Don't concern yourself. The rest is up to us."

"So be it," Tonah answered. "I must rest. I am confident that you will succeed. I will purge my mind of worry."

"Just take it easy. Things will be better soon." Caleb replied, rising to leave the room. I wish I felt as confident, he thought. Kaibito is a madman. He will kill Shanni before he'll let her go. He had to find a way to rescue her before Porter rode Kaibito to ground.

Chapter 20

"Well, we're in for a chase!" Porter gazed to the west as he spoke. Caleb and Manuelito stood beside him on the knoll and all that met the eye was desolation. The land fell away in great slashes, like gullies ripped from the earth by a giant claw. Three days had passed, hot and unbroken by clouds or rain. The sun beat down, marking their trail with long shadows that left no sign of their passage. They had found water at Chinle Wash and now they took their bearings from Carson Mesa to the south. The great Black Mesa reared to the southwest.

"Where do you think Kaibito's headed, Manuelito?" Porter asked.

"Difficult to tell. He knows all the Navaho lands and soon he will need to stop and rest. He will make for grass and water."

Porter chewed thoughtfully on a plug of tobacco. "Then I expect he has a far piece to go. This is as desolate a place as I've seen. Nothing here to look forward to."

"There is a place of water and grass that was home to the Ancient Ones. It is called Betatakin."

"How far?"

"Two days' ride, maybe more, due west."

"Might as well get on with it, then." Porter led down to where the men were waiting. They rode out single file, with Porter, Caleb and Manuelito in the lead. The country opened into desert valleys surrounded by weathered mesas.

The valleys were deceptive. They rode for hours without appearing to progress towards the hills to the west. Everything was on a giant scale, dwarfing the riders, and nowhere was there water. The scouts swept in wide circles, looking for sign of Kaibito's passage.

As they progressed, the mesas gave way to sheer rock formations, rising out of the valley floor like giant monuments to extend hundreds of feet into the air, silent sentinels timeless and foreboding, oblivious to the passage of man.

Time dragged for Caleb as he worried about Shanni. Was Kaibito mistreating her? He felt jealousy and rage welling up in him. They could not push the horses faster in the heat, but Caleb felt impatient and helpless. As they crept forward in the afternoon sun, he was tortured by his thoughts.

They made dry camp in the evening and the tired troopers were soon asleep. Night guards were placed out as a precaution, but Manuelito did not expect an attack. Kaibito would attempt to wear down his pursuers by hard travel.

The next day they topped out at Marsh Pass, confirming Manuelito's belief that Kaibito was bound for Betatakin.

Two of the scouts galloped back toward the column. Manuelito rode out to meet them and the three were engaged in earnest conversation when Caleb and the others caught up.

"What is it?" Porter asked, slapping dust from his uniform with his hat.

"The trackers say Kaibito's group turned off early, up one of the canyons," Manuelito replied. "We don't know if it is a trap, or if he knows of another way to Betatakin."

"Or if he's going someplace besides Betatakin."

Porter turned the possibilities over in his mind. If it was a ploy to draw them off the track, they could lose days in the maze of canyons and be in real trouble without water. On the other hand, if they did not stay close on Kaibito's trail, he could slip away.

"How much farther to Betatakin?"

"Half a day's ride, no more."

"You know for sure there's grass and water?"

"Yes."

"Then we gamble and head there. If Kaibito doesn't show, we will backtrack after the horses are fed and watered. He's got to come to ground somewhere. His horses can't last without water."

Despite his impatience, Caleb saw the wisdom of Porter's decision. The horses were all in. They would have to be rested for the final push.

Tension rose in Caleb as they bypassed the canyon Kaibito had taken. Shanni was so close, and now they were moving away.

They passed canyon after canyon. Manuelito signaled and they turned up a canyon no different than several they had passed. Caleb marveled that the Navaho could navigate in this featureless land.

As they progressed, desert scrub began to appear, and farther up, tinges of green portended grass. They drew near to bushes and small aspens that wound along a dry watercourse, their roots tapping the water underneath. Caleb's tired eyes drank in the beauty of the tiny park, an oasis of life in the dry country.

They continued past the aspens and the park widened. Looming above in the face of the granite cliff was an immense, semicircular opening forming a natural cavern. Inside was a city of stone and mortar. Hundreds of openings stared vacantly into the canyon.

Manuelito halted and pointed, "Betatakin."

"First things first," Porter responded. "Take us to where we can get at water, and we'll put out a defensive perimeter. Then we'll worry about finding Kaibito."

They had ridden past the giant opening to Betatakin when a rifle shot broke the stillness further up the canyon.

"Advance with caution," Porter ordered.

The troopers pulled rifles, forming a skirmish line, and advanced. As they rounded the corner of the canyon, they saw the body of a scout lying in the dry wash. Manuelito and the other scout were crouched behind boulders, looking up the canyon.

Manuelito answered Porter's silent question. "Kaibito got here first, and he controls the water."

Chapter 21

Shanni heard the sounds of battle and guessed the soldiers had attacked. She was caught up in the confusion as one of Kaibito's men had bound her hands and threw her astride a horse.

As they galloped up the canyon, she looked in vain for sign of the Huastecs. The area around the mine was abandoned. Fear and concern rose in her. Had Kaibito killed Tonah and the others? There was no time to think. She held on to the racing horse as Kaibito's men dynamited an exit and the band rode hard, traveling far into the night.

At last they stopped. Shanni was given water and she fell into an exhausted sleep. Before dawn she was awakened and the flight resumed. She lost track of the hours, but judged by Kaibito's pace that they were being pursued. Shanni felt a surge of hope. It could only be the soldiers! Let them come, she thought. If only they would catch up and kill Kaibito. She realized that she had changed. She had learned to hate. That's what they've done to me, she thought.

The band continued westward across a wide valley and into more canyons filled with talus and broken rock. The riders were forced to dismount and lead the horses. Near dusk, they topped the mesa and rode across a narrow stretch to descend into the adjoining canyon. Shanni saw trees, so green and out of place in the wilderness that they stunned the eyes. A rider lifted her from the horse and she was placed among the women and children of Kaibito's camp. They were given water, and then escorted up the steep trail to the stone dwellings nestled at the base of the cliffs. Hosta and the other women began to make cook fires and prepare the evening meals.

Kaibito was distracted now, but Shanni knew that once his preoccupation with the pursuers passed, he would come for her. She was on her own, there was no one left to rescue her.

She began scanning the camp area, looking for some means to defend herself.

A shot rang out down the canyon. Time was running out.

Porter was in a bad spot and he knew it. Kaibito was fighting on home ground and was well placed for defense. In addition, he controlled the water. Without access to water, Porter knew he could not outlast Kaibito in a siege, but a frontal assault would decimate his remaining troopers. He had run Kaibito to ground but he could not complete the kill. He had to do something now and there was only one alternative open to him.

"It's a Mexican standoff," he said to Caleb and Manuelito, who stood nearby holding the reins of their horses.

"We cannot attack without taking heavy losses, and they can't attack for the same reason. They'll want to stay and rest and water the horses. We've got to move before things get worse for us. It's risky, but we'll have to mount a night attack."

Caleb thought a moment. He understood the urgency, but night fighting with renegades in their own territory was bad business.

"They know the canyon. They'll have the advantage."

"Mano?"

"My scouts and I will go in first. We know this kind of fighting and can get in close. Your men follow. Once surprise is lost, it must be over very quickly."

"All right," Porter nodded. "Gather around, men, this is what we're going to do."

Past midnight Manuelito led out on foot to mount the attack. Porter pulled the horses well back and hitched them for the night. If Kaibito had spies out, they would report that the troopers were settling in until daybreak.

Caleb joined Manuelito as he led his men on foot to mount the attack. They crept through the trees like shadows, to reach the pool of water lying against the cliff face.

Manuelito motioned to halt and he disappeared into the darkness. Caleb heard a soft thud and saw the pale outline of a sentry as he collapsed to the ground. We've drawn first blood, he thought. Now we've got to move fast. They clambered up the slope, reaching Kaibito's men sleeping behind the screen of broken talus at the base of the cliff. A hoarse scream, cut off by

Manuelito's knife, raised the alarm. Despite the element of surprise, Kaibito's hardened fighters came to their feet, rifles blazing. Porter realized he had too few men to surround them. It was fight and win or die.

Caleb whirled at a silent form, his knife striking home. The renegade fell without a sound. Caleb was running among the fighting men, slashing, reacting, as he sought to reach the camp and find Shanni. Shots were ringing down from the dwellings as Caleb ran along the base of the cliff. That must be where they'd kept the women and children. Shanni would be there.

He fought his way up the stone steps to reach the camp, watching for the rear guard that was raining rifle fire down upon Porter's troops. He gained the last few steps and rolled over to cover as bullets spanged into the rock nearby. He saw the muzzle flash of the rifle in a doorway, and scrambled to reach the wall of the dwelling.

Caleb risked a quick glance into the open window. Women and children were hovering around a small fire, and among them was Shanni.

Caleb crawled forward along the wall to take out the rifleman. As he reached the doorway to swing his knife, he realized the man had disappeared. He looked inside and recognized Chama, who had stepped back to reload.

Their eyes met, and Chama reacted, casting aside the useless rifle to grab his knife and leap at Caleb. Caleb parried the thrust as he heard Shanni's sharp cry of recognition in the background. He and Chama rolled into the shadows as he fought to control Chama's knife hand. Chama was strong and skilled at knife fighting, and Caleb felt streaks of pain as Chama sliced, seeking a killing blow.

Chama disengaged and rolled to his feet, twisting to stab viciously as Caleb climbed to his feet. Caleb slashed out, burying his knife in Chama's bicep. Chama shrieked with pain, seizing his knife in the other hand to catch Caleb stretched out of position.

Caleb saw movement behind Chama. Shanni leaped forward, stabbing out with the knife she had hidden in the folds of her skirt. Chama grimaced and cried out, turning as the knife drove home.

Caleb charged, his knife catching Chama high up. Without a sound, Chama slipped to the ground. Caleb grabbed Shanni's hand and pulled her away.

"This way. No time." He whispered as they raced along the wall in the darkness.

His movements were sluggish, and he was covered with blood. Had Chama's knife found its mark?

A man loomed out of the shadows and seized Shanni. Her scream faded in his consciousness as he collapsed to the plaza. He lay for long moments trying to regain his strength.

Manuelito appeared and Caleb reached out, trying to steady himself. He tried to tell Manuelito to help Shanni but he could not make himself understood, and then he was falling into blackness.

Chapter 22

The travel had been long and arduous. Jorge Tupac welcomed the sight of his destination, hidden in the subtropical forest. He pressed through the dense vegetation, leading the burro. There was no trail so that he was required to wind among the vines and tree roots that blocked his path. He reached what appeared to be a knoll covered with vegetation rearing out of the forest. He knew the ancient Mayan temple he sought lay hidden beneath the forest cover.

He searched until he found the circular stone door covering a hidden passageway. Leaving the burro, he rolled the stone aside and entered. He found dry torches on a ledge and lit one with the cigar he had lit from his campfire hours ago.

As the torch flared, a bias relief depicted the history of the Mayans going back thousands of years, but Jorge had seen the mural before and he was in a hurry.

He shuffled along the passage to enter a circular stone chamber with a domed ceiling. In the center a raised stone alter supported a large crystal.

As he entered, light from his torch lit the chamber with ghostly shadows, flickering across the life-sized stone statues of gods that lined the walls, facing inward toward the crystal. The crystal absorbed the dim light, breaking it into a rainbow of colors, and then refracted it outward to illuminate the faces of the statues. The eyes of the statues began to glow softly.

Jorge's heart raced with apprehension. He did not want to be here. His mentor, long dead, had brought him to the temple as an apprentice and warned him to utilize its powers only in times of great need. Much power resided in this place. The forces that could be unleashed were beyond understanding, but Jorge was desperate and had to take the risk.

He heard a low rumble and looked up as a round window in the ceiling opened to permit sunlight to enter and strike the crystal. The crystal intensified the light, drawing power from the sun, and focused it on the statue facing Jorge.

As the stone warmed, the eyes slowly opened and blinked. Terror overcame Jorge as the eyes focused on him. What had he done? He wanted to flee but his feet were planted. He felt a voice speaking inside his head.

"For what purpose have you awakened me?"

Jorge summoned his strength to answer.

"People from our past are approaching. They are using the ancient powers to seek the Center. According to my mandate as a sentinel, I assembled my group to stop them. Their leader used the powers to defeat us. I was almost killed."

"So the time has come. The disloyal priests left enclaves hidden to rise against us in their future. These people must be stopped."

"I seek help. My sentinels are not strong enough to defeat them alone."

"So be it. You are authorized to contact the guardians for assistance."

"They are on a higher dimension. How will I reach them?"

"Project your awareness. The crystal will guide you."

The eyes closed as the light on the stone face faded. Jorge realized the stone god was only a conduit, or representation, of the presence that had spoken. The presence could be anywhere in the universe.

He shivered with fear but dared not flee. His mentor had warned him during his training that there was no place to hide. If he disobeyed his charge as a sentinel he would be found and destroyed. He felt the warm glow of light from the crystal covering his face as it widened to envelope his body. His apprehension faded and he felt like he was floating on a cloud with a sense of well-being and ease. His awareness heightened as the light dimmed and he found himself running along a narrow tunnel. He did not know the reason he felt a sense of urgency.

Bright sunlight hurt his eyes as he emerged to join a colony of animals feeding on a grain bin, and realized his awareness had been directed into the body of a rat. A large male scurried over and sniffed at him suspiciously.

Jorge gathered his strength and spoke with indignation. "I was ordered to find the guardians."

"And so you shall. What brings you?"

"A threat from the ancient times beyond the powers of the sentinels to stop."

"Come with me."

Jorge followed as the rat scurried across the floor and entered another maze of tunnels. They traveled a long distance to emerge in rock talus in a desert canyon. Five rats were waiting, resting silently in the shade of a cactus.

"Are you the guardians?" Jorge asked.

"We represent the guardians in this dimension. We chose this species to facilitate our meeting. Tell us what you seek."

Jorge became exasperated. Surely with their powers they knew of the threat and his attempts to stop it. There was no time to waste. They should be mounting a defense.

"Do not be impertinent!" A new voice spoke inside Jorge's head. "We have grave matters in many worlds to attend to. We will decide what is urgent here."

Jorge shrank back, chastened. Even his thoughts were not his own. He swallowed his fear and waited. He "felt" the guardians conversing silently but could not follow their thoughts. He had a sense they were debating the challenge methodically, without emotion. He would have felt the emotion.

The voice spoke again. "We have examined your memory of events. It appears that only one person used the powers of the ancients, but others with him have the potential. He must be eliminated before he can pass the skills on to those other individuals. As the sentinel, you must lead the charge."

"I tried," Jorge protested, "And I was almost killed."

"You were unwise to engage your adversary without determining the extent of his powers. Do not make that mistake again!"

"I came here seeking assistance, not condemnation."

"And you shall have it. One of the guardians will go with you and develop the plan of attack. He will be able to call upon our powers at will."

Jorge started to acquiesce when he heard the voice again. "Wait."

Jorge's awareness merged with the others as their group awareness expanded out and up to look down on the surreal scene of desert, rocks and cactus. Jorge saw the bodies of the rats they had inhabited a moment before, motionless below. The group awareness narrowed its focus and moved toward an owl that perched almost hidden in a cactus overlooking the clearing.

Jorge felt an alien awareness in the owl as it turned its eye toward them and blinked, sensing their presence.

"Tonah!" Jorge shouted silently, disrupting the group awareness as fear and anguish from his previous encounter with Tonah overcame him.

The owl launched a quick dive and sank its sharp talons into one of the rats below, sending the others scurrying for cover.

Jorge felt strong negative emotion blast him as the guardian seized control and beamed a powerful force at the presence in the owl.

But Tonah had disengaged. Only the owl remained, confused, to pick at its prey in the branches of the cactus.

"You have failed twice," the voice said with grim calmness. "We will augment your powers, but at the next level of engagement your failure will mean your death. See that you succeed."

"But..." Jorge started to protest when he felt his awareness shift to race along the dark tunnel into the room with the stone crystal. He became aware of a low rumble as the ceiling closed, shutting out the sunlight. He was alone with his torch.

Fighting panic, he stumbled to the exit and rolled the stone door back into place. Perspiring from fear and the heat, he went looking for the burro.

TONAH AWAKENED TO look across the plaza at the campfires of the Huastecs. Time was short and somehow he must engage Caleb and Shanni in the defense against the Guardians. He was no longer strong enough to do it alone, and soon they would have to face the Guardians without him.

Darkness surrounded Caleb as he stood listening, trying to get his bearings. An unpleasant stench of stagnant water reached his nostrils. He was in a damp and dangerous place he could not see. His hand moved to his revolver but the holster was empty. A faint glow reached his eyes and he blinked. The outline of a robed man began to appear and Caleb felt an unworldly primordial fear. He resisted the impulse to turn and run. What might he fall into in the darkness? The figure raised its head to gaze at Caleb, but he could only see an intense blue light where the eyes should have been. The light intensified, enveloping Caleb in a field of heated energy. He gasped and fell to his knees. Not since he was a boy had he felt such helpless terror. Caleb tried to rise, to fight back, but the energy was raw and ruthless, overpowering him. He screamed with rage and frustration.

As the sound of his scream echoed away, he heard a calm voice.

"Stop."

As Caleb peered through the cocoon of energy, he dimly saw Tonah, standing in the shadows. Tonah's hands were cupping the energy, deflecting it like a liquid stream back to the man-figure in the shadows. The energy writhed and crackled as it circled on itself. Multi-colored sparks flew outward as the figure, startled, swept an arm across its eyes and drew back sharply. The energy suddenly ceased, leaving Caleb gasping for breath. A strong odor of ozone permeated the air.

"Go home. Now!" Tonah commanded.

Where am I? Caleb thought, confused. And where is home?

He tried to question Tonah, but Tonah shook his head and extended a hand. As Caleb reached out, an intense shock accompanied by a flash of light reverberated throughout his body. He felt himself float freely. An all-encompassing compassion enveloped him with a sense of calm and well-being. He felt a presence encouraging him to let go and trust. If he would let go, he would be free of all the years of strain, of struggle and his cares would disappear.

This must be what it feels like to die, Caleb thought, easy and very peaceful. Death was something to embrace and not to fear.

"Not yet!" Tonah's voice reached him faintly. "Fight it. It is a trap. Do not give in. *Will* yourself to live!"

Deep inside Caleb a spark of fear ignited a return to reality. He was yielding to his own death! He reacted violently to free himself from the enfolding darkness.

Caleb awakened with a splitting headache and looked around to get his bearings. A corpsman held a canteen to his lips and he

115

James Gibson

drank. The man hurried away as Caleb raised his head to find
that he was with the troop near the base of Betatakin.

Lieutenant Porter hurried over with the corpsman.

"Easy, Caleb. You had us worried. You lost some blood, but
your wounds aren't that bad. For some reason you were slipping
into a coma and the corpsman was worried you might not make
it. Maybe you hit your head when you fell."

Caleb checked his wounds. He would have some scars but
none of the wounds were crippling. He had been lucky.

"How'd we make out?"

"We've broken the back of Kaibito's fighting force.
Leastways we fought them to a standstill. Kaibito and a few of his
men managed to slip away but they're on the run now for sure."

"And Shanni?"

"Kaibito took her with him I'm sorry to say. Why, I don't
know unless he hopes to use her as a bargaining chip."

"With whom?"

"With you, I'd guess."

"Why? All I want is Shanni. If he had left her, he would be
free of me."

"Well, I talked to Manuelito about that. He says Kaibito is
not straight in the head anymore. Keeping Shanni is one more
way for him to strike back at us white men, and Kaibito now has
a personal vendetta against you. You escaped from his camp,
freed the Huastecs, and killed Chama. Kaibito won't rest until he
has you staked out in the sun to die, and Shanni is his bait."

"What do you plan to do?"

"I don't have much choice. A number of my men are
wounded and now there are prisoners to see to. I'll have to ride
north to Goulding's trading post, about a day's ride from here.
We'll rest up until we are able to ride back to Fort Wingate.
What about you?"

"I'm going after Shanni."

"Ahuh. I figured as much. I can let you have a horse and
supplies and wish you luck. That's the best I can do."

"It's enough, and thanks. Where's Manuelito?"

"Tending to his men. I'll ask him to stop by."

Later Manuelito walked over to Caleb, his tall frame showing
cuts and bruises of battle. Manuelito must ache as much as I do,

Caleb thought, but you'd never know it by the way he ignores it.

"Did Porter tell you I intend to continue after Shanni?"

Manuelito nodded. "I wish I could go with you, but my men need care and I have been absent too long from my people. Kaibito is not dead, and as long as he lives he is now a threat to me and to the Navaho. In my own time and in my own way I must deal with him."

"And I must rescue Shanni."

"Kaibito has turned south, away from the trails of the white men. You will need a tracker. I will send Walpi with you, but he cannot go beyond the lands of the Navaho. Beyond there, you must do what you must do alone."

Caleb nodded his understanding. Manuelito wanted to help, but the treaty with the government required his warriors to remain on the reservation. He could not do anything to jeopardize his people.

The next morning, Caleb and Walpi split off from the troop and rode south. Walpi was a good tracker, Caleb noted. He circled widely and soon found the faint trace of Kaibito's trail as he retreated. The thought of Shanni with Kaibito drove Caleb, and they rode fast despite Caleb's discomfort from his wounds. The second day they crossed the Little Colorado River and discovered the remains of Kaibito's campfire. He was hardly a day ahead. There appeared to be six riders remaining in his party, plus Shanni. Kaibito was moving fast, making no attempt to hide his trail.

Noon of the third day, Walpi pulled his horse to a halt as they reached the border of the Navaho lands. Caleb thanked him with a handshake. Walpi had helped him close the gap. Now he must go on alone.

As Caleb rode, his headache returned to remind him of the nightmare. It had seemed as real as now, when he was awake. Memory of the fear returned. He had faced down fear as he fought in life and death confrontations. But the fear in the dream had been different, a terror that came from the depth of his being. It was the hopelessness of being out of control, of having no way to fight back, of facing overpowering and all-encompassing evil.

117

As soon as he rescued Shanni, he must return to Tonah and seek an explanation. What was he fighting? And how must he fight to successfully defeat this new threat?

The faint trail climbed out of the desert into highland meadows and forests of pine. The air grew cooler with altitude, and Caleb welcomed the greenery that gave respite from the barren grayness of the desert.

As the forest thickened, Caleb became increasingly apprehensive. He could not see far ahead, and the evergreens provided ideal cover for ambush. He slowed the horse and worked forward, senses alert. As he crossed a small stream and started up the glade, he found fresh hoof prints and his spirits lifted. He was gaining on Kaibito and his riders.

He leaned over his saddle, studying the tracks when the angry snap of a bullet passed overhead, followed by the sound of the rifle shot somewhere ahead. Caleb grabbed his rifle and rolled from the saddle. He scrambled to a nearby boulder as another shot sprayed gravel near him. He glimpsed the muzzle blast from the rifle, and levered two quick shots in that direction. He had the location fixed as he ran among the evergreens to close on his attacker.

He saw a flurry of movement ahead and saw his assailant grabbing for a horse. Caleb halted to aim as the rider turned and their eyes met. The rider raised his rifle and fired at Caleb, hurrying his shot and spoiling his aim. Caleb calmly squeezed off a return shot that dropped the rider from the saddle.

Caleb levered another round into the chamber and advanced carefully. The man was one of Kaibito's riders and he was dead. That's one, Caleb thought grimly, and now for the others.

Caleb was wary and his progress slowed. Kaibito was close enough to hear the shots, and would know when his rider did not return that Caleb was still on his trail. Now it was a matter of who made the first mistake.

Caleb broke out of the forest onto a point of land and wheeled his horse, startled. He was on the edge of a precipice where the land fell away sheer for thousands of feet. Deep canyons extended outward like giant fingers to the horizon. Weathered peaks broke the vista, rising like monoliths in wave after wave. He saw the tops of pines trees below on the slopes. In the distance, a faint blue stream between sheer canyon walls marked the passage of the Colorado River.

El Canon Grande! Kaibito had ridden into the depths of the Grand Canyon. This was trouble on top of trouble. As far as Caleb knew, Lee's Ferry to the northeast was the only crossing for hundreds of miles. A man could get lost in the canyon and die trying to find his way out.

Caleb nudged the horse and turned to follow a dim game trail down the long winding ridge. Halfway down he detected movement and paused to see the tiny specks of moving horses as Kaibito's band completed the descent and moved out of sight along the bank of the Colorado.

An hour later he reached the spot and followed the plain trail left by Kaibito's riders. The canyon narrowed. Caleb was forced to dismount and walk, leading the horse, along a trail that was little more than a ledge in places, inches from the roaring water of the Colorado. The river became swifter as the stream narrowed into rapids, trapped between the walls of the canyon. Farther along, the river widened with gravel shoals on both sides. Caleb saw where the riders had entered the water to cross over. He urged his horse forward to swim in the swift current. They struck the shore further down and the horse climbed out to shake off the water. Caleb feared attack and urged the horse to cover. The stillness was broken by a man's loud laughter reverberating off the canyon walls. Caleb pulled up short, startled. A horse was walking toward him, not a hundred yards away, and on the horse was Shanni!

Chapter 23

Shanni stood frozen with surprise as Caleb appeared in the doorway of the dwelling. She screamed as Chama attacked and the fight carried Caleb and Chama into the shadows. The din of battle below the plaza muffled the sound of their exertions. Shanni ran outside, staying in the shadows along the wall. Her foot touched a body, almost tripping her, and she recoiled. In the dim light she made out one of Kaibito's riders, dead. Steeling herself, she knelt down to search for a weapon. Her hand closed on a knife and she concealed it in the folds of her skirt as she rose and raced back to help Caleb. She found Caleb on his back, struggling to get to his feet as Chama drew back for a final blow. Without hesitation, she leaped forward, burying the knife in Chama's back. He stiffened, screaming, and started to turn. Caleb gained his feet and struck, burying his knife in Chama's chest. Chama crumpled soundlessly to the dirt floor.

Caleb grasped Shanni's hand and turned to flee the dwelling. They could hear people moving in the darkness as the battle reached the plaza.

A form detached from the shadows, and Shanni recognized Tovar, one of Kaibito's men as he struck Caleb a glancing blow from behind. Caleb collapsed, rolling away into the shadows as she tried to hold him up.

Tovar turned to Shanni.

"What's this?" he asked, seeking to twist her face around.

Shanni reacted violently, lashing out with the bloody knife. The knife struck with all her strength behind it, striking bone high in Tovar's chest. He screamed and staggered back, wrenching the knife hilt from her hand. He sagged to the dusty plaza.

Shanni stood numb, trying to wipe Tovar's blood off her hand. She had killed him. She felt cold rage inside and began to tremble.

Kaibito appeared and saw Tovar lying at Shanni's feet. Seizing her roughly, he dragged her up a narrow ledge with several of his men. They climbed steadily until they reached the top of the mesa and Shanni saw stars overhead. The smell of evergreens wafted on the air.

Kaibito led to the horses, dragging Shanni along. Kaibito turned, dark anger flashing in his eyes as he hit Shanni a slashing blow that staggered her back. She was semiconscious, tasting blood in her mouth as Kaibito threw her over the saddle and the men rode away from the scene of battle.

They rode all night, putting distance between themselves and Betatakin. At sunup, they stopped to eat and let the horses rest. There was little conversation from the tired men as Kaibito paced, anxious to be moving.

Shanni's eyes burned from lack of sleep as the landscape swam in front of her. Her tired gaze focused on a nearby rock as its shadows and irregular features seemed to move.

Her perception shifted and she saw Tonah's worried visage. "Follow me," he commanded. The rock expanded, filling her vision as she was drawn forward, enveloped by the shadows. She was in darkness with a damp, unpleasant odor overpowering her senses. As if in a dream, she could only watch helplessly as Caleb faced an unholy and evil presence.

"Watch and remember."

She felt Tonah's voice inside her head as the scene brightened. A flash of energy struck Caleb, smashing him to his knees. Shanni wanted to cry out but could not. She had the disorienting feeling that she was not "there", as if she were viewing the scene through a hidden veil. Tonah intervened, deflecting the energy as Caleb faded from view. The evil presence overwhelmed her, filling her with dread and loathing. Her prescience heightened and she felt the intent of the entity to end Caleb's life. She shook uncontrollably as she sought to break free and help Caleb before it was too late.

"Go now, but remember."

Her awareness returned to the rock and Shanni felt the landscape swim back into view. What had happened to Caleb? Had Tonah been strong enough to save him? A terrible resolve grew in Shanni. She lived in an evil world. She must find Tonah and learn how to combat this evil.

They rode all day in the blistering sun, but Shanni was only dimly aware of her surroundings. Her heightened awareness coupled with her gift of prescience rolled out potential futures from which she, Caleb and Tonah must chose and, once chosen, that they must fight to make a reality. Otherwise, they faced a future of disaster for themselves and the Huastecs.

As they camped for the night, Kaibito seemed more relaxed. He was satisfied with their progress and the scouts' reports of lack of pursuit. Shanni faced her situation coldly. Kaibito had escaped and could do with her as he willed. She had no weapons and Kaibito knew that she had killed Tovar. What would he do?

After the meal, Kaibito walked over, his eyes piercing as he looked down at her.

"So the little dama has dirtied herself, spilling blood like a common street wench."

"How does it feel?" he taunted. "You are no better than I or any one of us who has killed to survive. Now you are bait, nothing more. Your man Caleb is on our trail, and this time he will not escape. You will watch him die slowly, stretched out in the sun, and then my men will share you. They deserve a reward and you will treat them well, for when they tire of you, you will share the white-eye's fate."

Mohon, one of Kaibito's riders stood nearby, amused at the byplay. As Kaibito walked away, Mohon grasped Shanni's hair, pulling her head back painfully. A knife flashed in his hand. Shanni stifled a scream as the cold blade touched her throat. Mohon laughed and started to pull the knife away.

Rage replaced surprise as Shanni turned, eyes flashing. Without thinking, she focused her will and seized the knife in a vortex of energy that turned his hand to slash downward viciously. Mohon screamed in surprise and horror as the knife embedded itself in his thigh, thick blood spurting from the wound.

Kaibito and the other riders came running at the disturbance.

"What happened?" Kaibito demanded.

"She's a witch!" Mohon screamed, writhing in pain. "She stabbed me!"

"He stabbed himself," Shanni shot back. "I never touched him."

"Did she touch your knife?" Kaibito asked, looking at Mohon.

"No, but somehow she forced the knife into my leg!"

"Take care of that wound, and stay away from her. And quit chewing that mescal! If you can't ride, we'll leave you behind!"

The riders helped Mohon move away to bandage his wound. Kaibito looked at her a moment, puzzled, and then returned to the campfire.

Shanni scolded herself. She must not reveal her abilities until it counted. She was vulnerable now, without protection even from Kaibito. Caleb was on their trail and he must come soon.

The next day they crossed the Colorado River and Kaibito turned, smiling.

"Your man Caleb is anxious. He drives himself to catch up with us. One of my riders slowed him a little, but soon he will arrive and we will begin our sport."

Shanni saw the madness in Kaibito's eyes. Caleb was being lured into a trap. She must find a way to warn him. They rode up from the river into a dense grove of pine and cedar. Hidden from view, Kaibito dismounted and the men took up posts to watch the river. When Caleb appeared, Kaibito dragged her off the horse and clasped a rude hand across her mouth. Shanni started to struggle, but Kaibito drew back his fist and she stopped. She knew what he would do.

She watched as Caleb halted and searched the surroundings, and then swam his horse across the river. He emerged, wet and disheveled, on the shoals further down.

Kaibito turned to her.

"Now you will see the genius of Kaibito. Caleb Stone wants you so badly; I will give you to him. Tell him I said the only way he can save his life is to return you to me. We will see what choice he makes."

"He won't believe you." Shanni answered.

"It doesn't matter. He cannot escape, and he'll have to kill you for you to escape your fate with me."

Kaibito lifted her into the saddle and slapped the horse away down the slope as she grasped for the loose reins.

Kaibito's laugh pealed off the walls of the canyon as Caleb looked up and saw her approaching.

"Run, Caleb! It's a trap! They'll kill you".

Caleb spurred up to catch the horse and turned, lifting her into his arms.

The canyon became quiet. Only the water of the Colorado broke the stillness.

Kaibito appeared followed by two of his riders. Caleb wheeled the horses, looking back across the river. Another rider emerged from behind a wall, blocking the way back across the river.

"You'll have to leave me, Caleb, and save yourself," Shanni said. "Kaibito said he would spare you if you left me. It's your only chance and Tonah and the Huastecs need you."

Caleb turned to look at her, realization of Kaibito's mad game showing in his face. Rage overcame him as he saw what Kaibito was trying to do.

"The hell with Kaibito!" he exploded, slapping Shanni's horse into a run down the narrow canyon.

Kaibito's whoop of excitement rang in their ears as the horses leapt into the unknown chasm of the Colorado.

Chapter 24

They rode across an expanse of land that shoaled into the river. The canyon wall loomed overhead, casting dark shadows as the ledge narrowed. Caleb saw that the path was running out and they were trapped. He whirled to lever shots from his rifle at Kaibito and his men. Answering shots peppered gravel under his horse as he spun around to follow Shanni.

They rounded a corner and found the sheer walls came up to the rushing water, blocking their progress.

"Into the water," Caleb shouted over the roar of the river.

They spurred the frightened horses forward, and they plunged heavily into the river. The horses sank deep, and then fought to the surface, caught up in the swift current. Caleb and Shanni slipped from the saddles to clutch saddle straps, freeing the horses to swim. The churning water hurled them forward as they spun around and around, out of control.

Caleb heard the ominous roar of approaching rapids reverberating off the stone cliffs as the channel narrowed. They had to find a way out of the water.

Caleb looked around desperately for a way out, but the river ran between sheer walls. They were at the mercy of the river. The river swept around a corner and they approached the rapids. Boulders lifted out of the water, creating a cauldron of white water. Shanni's horse was carried broadside into a large rock and Caleb heard the sound of ribs breaking. Shanni was thrown clear and Caleb reached out for her as he swept by.

They were whirling from one channel to another through the current, gasping for the next mouthful of air through the spray. Caleb lost his grip on the horse as he fought the water and held onto Shanni.

Caleb lost track of time as numbness from the cold water seeped through him. His limbs became heavy and he knew they must get out of the water before they drowned.

The river widened in a bend carrying Caleb and Shanni wide toward the far shore. Caleb felt his boots grate on the gravel bottom. Kicking with his last strength, he dragged Shanni toward the shallow sand bank before the current could carry them past the landing. He sprawled, semi-conscious and spent, trying to catch his breath.

Shanni coughed beside him, and he turned to see clear water pouring from her mouth. He lifted her to a sitting position, and she drew a deep breath, clearing her lungs.

Caleb surveyed their surroundings. They were safe for the present. His horse stood nearby, head down with fatigue. Shanni's horse had been swept away.

Shanni's lips were blue from the cold and shock. He put his arm around her and helped her to a small ledge under the overhanging cliff.

"Sit here, in the sunlight," Caleb said. "The sun will help warm you."

Caleb walked to the horse and secured a tin of matches Porter had included with supplies in the saddlebags. He gathered dry driftwood and soon had a small, hot fire blazing.

"Shanni, we've got to dry our clothes and get warm. I'm afraid I don't have anything for a wrap. The saddle blanket is soaked."

Shanni looked up, deep circles of fatigue under her eyes. She stood up and turned her back. She began undressing, the sun golden on her damp skin. Her garments fell to the ground and she stooped to retrieve them as she turned. Her eyes met Caleb's, as she stood erect, her breasts lifted, and handed him the clothing.

Caleb took the garments and spread them on sticks near the fire to dry. Shanni turned her back to the sun and sat down as Caleb undressed and added his clothes to the stack steaming from the heat of the fire. Later, warmed by the fire and cheered by dry clothes, they explored the narrow strip of sand along the river. There was little vegetation and no source of food.

Caleb felt hunger gnawing at him. "We might as well go on," he said. "Nothing to help us here."

Shanni nodded, but did not attempt to get up. Caleb saw that she was all in.

"I'm sorry, maybe we'd better rest longer. Guess I'm too anxious to get moving."

"I'm all right. We can go on. I was just thinking of how happy I am with you. I don't want us to be apart ever again."

Caleb reached out as she stood up, her arms slipping under his as they held each other, her face on his chest.

Shanni took a deep breath and stepped back.

"I want us to be married, soon. I do not trust the world anymore and I'm afraid. Too much has happened. I don't want to wait."

"That's what I want, too. With you as my wife I'll be happy."

He mounted the horse and swung Shanni up behind him. He nudged the horse forward to climb out of the canyon. They needed food, shelter, and fresh horses, and Kaibito was still on their trail.

Chapter 25

Taking his direction from the sun, Caleb rode north, a direction he knew would take them out of the Colorado canyon into the highlands of Utah. His plan was to intercept a branch of the Old Spanish trail and follow it east to Lee's Ferry. There they could get supplies and horses, and proceed two days' ride to Goulding's trading post to link up with Porter. If Porter had already gone, they could ride southeast to Manuelito's camp and the Huastecs.

As they rode, Shanni broke the silence.

"Back there I told you I am afraid. It's more than Kaibito. Have you noticed anything strange lately?"

"Strange, like what?"

"Like nightmares?"

Caleb paused. How did she know?

"Well, I had a rough time after the battle. Porter said they thought I was going into a coma."

"What did you experience?"

"I dreamed I was being attacked by a man in shadows. Tonah appeared to deflect the attack, and then I felt a pleasant, peaceful sensation, like I was floating. Tonah broke in and warned me to fight it or I would die. Then I woke up in Porter's camp."

"I was in your dream as an observer. I could watch but could not intervene."

"How could that be? I never heard of two people sharing the same dream."

"Three people, for Tonah shared the experience also. It was not a dream."

"What could it be but a dream?"

"Didn't it seem real?"

"Yes, but then I woke up."

"And how did you feel?"

"Tired, exhausted, kind of disoriented."

"What you experienced was one of the other worlds Tonah spoke of. There we have enemies who seek to destroy us. That is why I am afraid. I fear them more than Kaibito."

"Kaibito has riders and guns. He's the one to fear. Dreams cannot kill us."

"Do not close your mind, Caleb. We must escape Kaibito and return to Tonah and then we must learn to fight our real enemies."

They rode in silence. Caleb did not want to argue, but he found Shanni's words disturbing. She had reminded him of the headaches, and the disorientation, but they could be explained. He'd been attacked and had lost blood; maybe he was even in mild shock.

Clearly she believed in Tonah's perceptions, but how could he?

Their travel took them across rugged canyon land, climbing through expanses of pine and cedar to reach the highlands of the Uinkaret Plateau. Caleb was alert for game, but the few deer he saw were too wary for him to get close enough for a shot from the revolver. That told him they had been hunted, and he became wary. He recalled that the Hualapai roamed the region.

They rode up a twisting canyon speckled with trees and underbrush and found a small stream. They stopped to drink, and then proceeded along the watercourse. Where there was water there would be game and they needed to eat.

The evergreens thinned and Caleb pulled up, peering at a knoll overlooking a dry wash. Set into the bank of the ridge, almost hidden, appeared to be some sort of dugout habitation. Caleb pulled the horse back to cover and dismounted. Motioning for Shanni to remain with the horse, he drew the revolver and scouted ahead on foot.

Up close, Caleb saw the dugout was cleverly hidden, its roof sodded with grass. It would have been invisible had he approached from another direction.

He eased closer, careful to keep the angle of the wash between himself and the doorway.

"Hello the cabin," he called softly. "Anybody home?"

He waited, and then a voice answered from a cluster of cedars behind him.

James Gibson

"At least ye speak English! What do ye want?"

Caleb froze. The voice was not Kaibito's, but he knew a gun was leveled on him. He slid the revolver back into the holster and turned slowly.

"We're lost and need help, food at least. We had trouble."

"I kin see that. Who's 'we'?"

"My woman and I. Renegade Navaho are after us. Now, who are you and will you help?"

"Maybe. Don't get impatient. Men die who move too quick out here."

Caleb waited, letting the man make up his mind.

A striking figure emerged from the thicket. The man was clothed in furs with a full beard covering his face. Long, unkempt hair hung about his shoulders as he watched Caleb with piercing black eyes. A wicked bowie knife, sheathed in a broad belt, completed the outfit.

"Name's MacLinn. Call your woman up and I'll dig out some grub."

MacLinn shuffled off into the woods while Caleb returned to get Shanni.

MacLinn returned with a deer haunch and set about slicing and roasting meat. He put on a pot of coffee and sat back smoking a pipe while Caleb and Shanni ate. Caleb finished and wiped grease from his hands on the dry grass.

"We're beholden to you. We'd been without awhile and that was fine eating. I hope we don't bring you trouble for it."

"How so?"

Caleb briefly explained the trouble with Kaibito and Shanni's rescue.

Amos listened attentively without interrupting, his eyes glistening with interest.

"Well," MacLinn said when Caleb finished. "You're a long way from home with rough country yet to travel. Me, I trapped this country for years. When the fur trade petered out, I stayed on. I like the country and the Indians don't bother me, but I'll take your warning about Kaibito. If he comes snooping around, I'll handle him. I ain't easily surprised."

"I can see that," Caleb laughed, remembering his approach to the cabin.

130

Shanni had finished eating and sat with her head on her knees. She was exhausted and Caleb felt drowsiness settling over him.

"You're all in," MacLinn observed. "Use my dugout to catch some sleep. I'll keep an eye out about and put some provisions together for you."

"That'll be fine, and thanks."

Caleb helped Shanni into the cool interior of the dugout. Furs spread over pine needles made a soft and aromatic bed. Clearly MacLinn liked his creature comforts. The room was small and Caleb was aware of Shanni's warm body next to him as he fell asleep.

Early the next morning they awakened refreshed and exited the dugout. MacLinn drifted in silently from the cedars and set about making breakfast. Shanni offered to help but MacLinn waved her away with a smile. Caleb savored the strong black coffee, wondering how MacLinn managed it this far from civilization.

As if reading his mind, MacLinn spoke up. "I like this life, open country to roam in and free to do as I please, but I do like a few things from civilization, like coffee and tobacco. I ride to Lee's Ferry on occasion and stock up. I use fresh grounds when I have company, which ain't often!"

MacLinn laughed heartily, his heavy frame shaking. Shanni's energy had returned with the sleep and the meal, and she set about helping clean up after breakfast.

"Here, no need for that," MacLinn protested. "I'll see to that later. Let's visit while we have the chance."

"Oh, I can visit while I clean up. I like to be busy."

MacLinn was suddenly silent, puffing on his pipe. Shanni perceived a sadness come over him. His eyes misted, lost in thought and far away. As if in a dream, she followed his memories to a time in his past. She felt waves of grief and sadness she did not understand. She stood frozen, unable to move.

"I feel a sadness in you," she said.

MacLinn's mind came back to the present, and his black eyes pierced Shanni's.

"Didn't know you could read minds," he said.

"I'm sorry. I didn't mean to offend."

"I'm not offended. Fact is, you remind me of my daughter. She moved in a certain way, like you do. Reckon that set me to remembering."

"But she's gone now?"

"Yes, for many years, both her and her mother. I killed the men that did it, but it couldn't bring them back. I did what I could."

"I'm sorry to remind you of painful days."

"Not your fault. Every man out here has a past, some good but most bad. Not sure where I fit."

"We're grateful for your help. I don't know how we can repay you."

"Don't worry about that. There's plenty that's helped me along the way. When the time comes, you pass it on. That's how life evens out."

"We're much obliged," Caleb stepped in to shake MacLinn's hand. "We've got to be moving. We don't know how close Kaibito may be on our trail."

"Remember the route I showed ye. It'll take ye oot and into Lee's ferry. Sorry I got no horse to lend ye."

"You've helped us more than enough. Until we meet again."

Shanni reached up to MacLinn to place a gentle kiss on his cheek.

"Thank you for being our friend," she said.

"And you, lassie."

Caleb mounted and swung Shanni up behind him.

"God speed." MacLinn called, and waved as they left the clearing.

They were descending in altitude and the going became easier for the horse. Caleb let it pick its way across open glades and through the cedar and pines that forested the slopes. The hours passed pleasantly as they covered miles while the sun moved to the west, casting long shadows that brought coolness to the air.

Caleb had started to relax when he was startled by the sound of a rifle shot ahead. He took cover and dismounted, motioning Shanni to stay as he drew his revolver and peered ahead.

"Don't shoot." The familiar voice of MacLinn called from the undergrowth. "'Tis only I, Amos."

MacLinn emerged from the undergrowth with a still body thrown carelessly across his massive shoulder. Caleb recognized one of Kaibito's riders and he was dead.

"Consider this a little present, lad and lassie," he said. "From ol' Amos MacLinn!"

"Amos," Caleb replied, "If you are ever in Mancos, Colorado, come to my ranch. The welcome mat will be out for you."

With a wave, Amos moved away, a stocky, furry apparition disappearing among the cedars. Caleb drew a deep breath and climbed back on the horse.

He lifted Shanni up, feeling her arms around him as he nudged the horse forward. Only three riders left now, he thought, and one of them is Kaibito.

Chapter 26

Caleb was wary. Kaibito would know where his men were scouting, and when one did not return, he would focus on that area.

The trail he followed was clearly marked by constant traffic by Mormons traveling from southern Utah to the crossing of the Colorado River at Lee's Ferry, near Page, in the Arizona Territory.

The first night they made camp at a water hole away from the trail that MacLinn had described. This gave some protection from Kaibito's men who would be watching the usual camping areas. The second day they reached a small Mormon settlement where Caleb traded for two fresh horses and a rifle, giving his marker for a draft on his bank, the usual practice in a country where a man's word was his bond and deals were made on a handshake.

With fresh horses and a rifle, Caleb felt better prepared to elude Kaibito, or to fight if need be, as he and Shanni rode away from the Mormon settlement.

Late in the afternoon, Caleb and Shanni heard riders approaching at a gallop. Caleb motioned Shanni to turn off the trail as the men pulled their horses to a halt a few hundred yards away.

Caleb recognized two of Kaibito's men at the same time they saw Caleb and Shanni. The riders pulled up rifles as Caleb spun, leading Shanni off the trail to the cover of a ravine.

The two riders spurred forward, weaving to avoid giving him a clean shot as they fired. Caleb fired twice and missed. They were good riders, leaning low over their horses as they approached to ride him down. Caleb's third bullet found its mark, lifting one of the riders in the saddle to fall limply into the coarse grass. The other rider found cover and was lost from sight.

Caleb motioned Shanni to stay with the horses as he crept forward on foot. He must deal with the gunman quickly. If

Kaibito was within hearing of the rifle shots, he and his remaining men could be riding to join him.

Perspiration from heat and exertion lined Caleb's forehead as he paused to listen, every nerve alert. Let the gunman make the first mistake.

The soft rustle of a leaf warned him and he moved in time to avoid a bullet that slapped into the foliage near his head. He levered two quick shots in the direction of the muzzle flash, and circled to cautiously approach the ambush site. He saw fresh blood spotting the grass. The wound would slow the gunman down, but make him more dangerous.

Caleb peered ahead, following the trail of blood that disappeared into the dense foliage. Moments later he heard the drum of hoof beats disappearing through the forest. Caleb ran up too late to get a shot at the fleeing rider.

The gunman would report to Kaibito and Kaibito would know where to find them, but it couldn't be helped now.

Caleb and Shanni walked to the dead rider. Shanni stared at the still form without emotion.

"We'd better take the horse and his rifle," Caleb said. "We'll need both if Kaibito and his men find us before we can get to Lee's Ferry."

They made dry camp at nightfall. Caleb knew they couldn't risk a fire with Kaibito and his men hunting them. Supper was spare, and Caleb missed having a cup of coffee.

"Not much to live on," he observed apologetically, as Shanni ate from the pack MacLinn had prepared.

"It's enough. I'm not very hungry."

"Sorry you had to see the dead rider back there."

"It was a relief to see him dead. I felt no remorse when I saw him. Before, the sight of death sickened me. Now I worry that I'm becoming insensitive to it."

"This is a violent land. I've seen my share of killing. To me it is kill or be killed, and I feel a man has to defend himself."

"That's not what I meant. As I become more insensitive, I am less able to see the dangers of the future. I am concerned my powers are diminishing, and I will be unable to help my people."

"We're under a lot of stress, not eating or sleeping, with Kaibito on our trail. You'll feel better when we get back to Tonah and your people."

"Yes, we must get back, and soon. Tonah can help me to find my way."

Caleb was struck by the strangeness of her words. Sometimes he did not understand her thinking, but he loved her and that was enough.

Shanni felt Caleb's thoughts, but avoided his glance as he turned to see to the horses. Was this violent country molding her into its image? Was she changing into someone different from the woman Caleb loved? Would he sense the change and be repulsed by her?

She felt the same foreboding she had sensed when Tonah went out to seek Kaibito's help. Had they come this far to find death after all? Tonah's vision had foretold they would not be killed, and she had begun to have hope again. But there were many unknowns in this strange and violent land, and even Tonah was not infallible.

Caleb was tired and sought his blanket early. Shanni stretched out to rest, but her mind was restless. She stared up at the timeless stars, trying to read her fate. After a while, fatigue became stronger than fear and sleep claimed her.

Lee's Ferry was little more than a way station supporting the ferry operation. Jed Baker, an enterprising Mormon, had seen the business potential of the crossing and installed a ferry. As traffic grew, his business had increased to provide meals, lodging and livery for travelers in the low buildings he'd built near the road.

Jed and his wives and children lived in a log house set well back among the pines. His long beard and soft voice gave him a gentle demeanor that belied his powerful frame. His constant contact with strangers had developed in him a quick and accurate assessment of men and their motives. He and his grown sons were always moving about, alert, quick to lend a hand, but somehow always in reach of their rifles. The Bakers' were neighborly, but nobody's fool. They survived and prospered in rough country.

Jed looked up from his work at the riders approaching down the trail. A man and woman were traveling without a packhorse. They'd had trouble, but then most strangers who came through had trouble.

Jed stepped out to greet Caleb and Shanni.

"My name's Jed Baker, and I run this ferry. Get down and rest. My boys will see to your horses."

"Reckon we're glad to be here at that. We're worn out."

"Some food and hot coffee is the place to start. Go on in and help yourself. After you've eaten, you'll feel better and we can talk."

Caleb nodded his agreement and helped Shanni down from her horse. She was tired but game, and walked ahead of him into the dim interior of the dining room.

Caleb and Shanni sat down to a rich stew with home made bread, coffee and water. The hot food was welcome after their cold fare and their spirits improved. "That may be the best meal I ever ate," Caleb observed as he sat back with the coffee.

Shanni smiled, "I'll know how to cook for you: just leave you out a couple of days before I feed you a hot meal!"

"I didn't see you holding back any, either."

"I was ravenous, and it's good stew."

Jed walked in, poured a cup of coffee and joined them. A couple of riders, dusty from travel, came in and took a seat in a corner to eat. Caleb's glance told him they were not Kaibito's men so he paid them no mind. It didn't pay to appear nosy with strangers.

"It was a fine meal, and much obliged," Caleb said to Jed. "And not a moment too soon. We were about all in."

"Glad you liked it. That's why we keep it on the stove. Most people are half-starved when they get here. You folks are welcome to stay the night."

"We'd like to, but you need to know we have some riders hunting us. "

"Most people know we don't abide trouble here, but I can't help you once you ride out."

"Fair enough."

Caleb and Shanni went to the sleeping quarters, separated by a partition. The clean sheets would be a luxury after the rigors of the trail, Caleb thought.

Caleb hung his gun belt within reach from long habit. He stretched out on the bed and relaxed as the fatigue of the trail caught up to him. In moments he was asleep.

Sometime during the night a slight noise disturbed his sleep and he roused, silently reaching for his gun.

A low voice spoke. "Don't."

Caleb froze as his eyes adjusted to the low light. He recognized one of the strangers from the previous evening, holding a Colt revolver near his face. At the man's motion, he began to dress. He could tell from quiet sounds across the partition that Shanni had also been awakened to prepare for travel.

They were hastened out a side door to waiting horses. The men led off quietly until they cleared the settlement and then they spurred the horses to a gallop.

Caleb glanced at the stars to get his direction and noted they were heading northeast, toward the San Juan River. That was rough, unsettled country with only Goulding's trading post as an enclave for white men.

They turned off the trail and were led into a small clearing containing a campfire reduced to coals. Two figures rose at their arrival and Caleb recognized Kaibito and Mohon! How far could Kaibito reach? Caleb wondered. How was he tied to these strangers?

Caleb saw a fresh bandage on Mohon's arm as Mohon cast a baleful glance in his direction. Mohon must have been the other rider on the trail, which meant Kaibito knew what had happened.

The strangers walked over to Kaibito, conversed in low tones, and then returned to Caleb and Shanni.

"Call me 'Wilson', and this is Long," the man said. "Better get some sleep. Tomorrow we go hunting for Spanish silver, and if you want the little woman to stay healthy, you'd better go direct."

So that was it, Caleb thought, glancing at Shanni. They knew of the Spanish coin cache. Caleb read the menace in Wilson's voice. He would not hesitate to torture Shanni to get at the silver. But where did Kaibito fit in, and if he took them to the silver, what then?

Caleb stretched out on his blanket and feigned sleep, but his mind was working, weighing possibilities and trying to develop a plan to address the unexpected turn of events.

Chapter 27

At Tonah's bidding, Matal entered the lodge and sat cross-legged, observing the obligatory moments of silence. Out of respect, he would wait for Tonah to speak first.

"Welcome, Matal. I perceive agitation in you today."

Matal nodded. While Tonah did not read minds, Matal knew his gifts often perceived the winds of emotion that blew through the psyches of those near him. Matal always felt a bit unsettled, as if Tonah perceived his intentions before he could speak.

"Yes," Matal answered. "The Huastec men and I have been discussing what to do. Shanni is in the hand of our enemies, and the soldiers, unable to catch Kaibito, are returning to the fort. Lieutenant Porter states that only Caleb Stone continues the pursuit of Kaibito."

"That is true. The soldiers returned from Goulding's trading post yesterday. They had no word on the fate of Caleb or Shanni."

"We have suffered from our lack of knowledge of modern weapons to fight our enemies, but we are learning." Matal continued. "We cannot rely on others to fight our battles. Six of us have decided to take our rifles and ride in search of Caleb and Shanni. We would like to go with your blessing."

Tonah studied Matal's words in silence. Matal and the young men had matured during the recent hardships, but were no match for Kaibito's men. The Huastecs could not afford to lose any more of their future warriors, but he read the determination in Matal's eyes. How could he deny them his support when they were willing to risk their lives?

"Where will you go? We do not know the land where they disappeared."

"Caleb had planned to rescue Shanni and, if successful, meet Porter at the trading post. Manuelito left one of his men there to watch for Caleb and Shanni. We will join him and he will scout for us if Caleb and Shanni have not appeared."

With all the unknowns, it was a good plan, Tonah thought. They had thought the plan through, and he understood Matal's need to take action. In recent days Tonah had wished his body were strong enough to ride to help, but now he was old and would have to help in other ways.

"Go," Tonah answered. "Go with my blessing and my prayers, but do not waste the lives of those you lead."

Matal nodded and rose, bowing in respect as he left the dwelling.

GOULDING'S TRADING POST was a fortress-like structure constructed of adobe, and set in a canyon near a spring. The spring had been a rendezvous site during the heyday of the fur trade, where trappers had convened to trade, swap stories, and fight. Goulding had foreseen the possibilities and settled, building the mercantile that served as a hub of activity for hundreds of miles of sparsely settled territory.

A constant stream of Anglo and Indian riders flowed through the trading post so that Manuelito's scout, Oljato, had been inconspicuous lounging about watching the traffic. So far he'd found no clue as to the whereabouts or fate of Caleb and Shanni.

He showed no sign of recognition when the dusty riders rode in from the south and bought supplies. As they remounted to ride out, the leader's glance swept the street and met Oljato's for an instant. Oljato nodded slightly, and walked casually to retrieve his horse and follow their trail.

Matal, waiting out of sight with his riders along the trail, hailed Oljato as he neared. "Manuelito told me I'd find you here. We've come to find Caleb and Shanni. We need your help in finding our way in this country."

Oljato nodded. He was impatient at waiting and felt the need to act. Even now events could be spinning out of control.

"A trader came in this morning with news that a couple was kidnapped by Anglos at Lee's Ferry, and I recall a stranger at the post a few days ago buying more supplies than one man could use. I'm guessing Caleb rescued Shanni, but then ran into more trouble."

"No sign of Kaibito or his men?"

"None."

Matal pondered the point. "Maybe it isn't Caleb and Shanni. Why would Anglos bother with them? We can't afford to lose time chasing in the wrong direction."

"I thought the same," Oljato answered, "Until the trader said the woman was Indian. There can't be many mixed couples riding through, and the time frame is about right for them to have ridden that far."

"You're right. We've got to make haste and find their trail."

Caleb glanced worriedly at Shanni as they followed their captors eastward along the San Juan River. Shanni had been listless and withdrawn since their capture, as if she had given up hope. They had come so far, she'd said, only to fall into Kaibito's hands again. Would they never be free of him?

They were a day's ride away from Goulding's trading post. Caleb had tried to think of a way to alert Porter when Wilson rode in for supplies, but he and Shanni had been kept well away from the post and he'd had no chance.

Wilson seemed familiar with the general area and set a brisk pace. He was all business, leading the group with military precision. Kaibito seemed content to lie back for the present. Both he and Mohon kept to themselves.

The third day they struck the Mancos River between high bluffs and Caleb realized with irony that he and Shanni were coming full circle, back to the ambush site where it had all started. Had it only been months ago? Certainly less than a year, and yet it seemed a lifetime ago. They had been caught up in events and swept along like the rapids of the Colorado, fighting and reacting to stay alive.

That night they camped along the Mancos, and after supper Wilson turned to Caleb and Shanni.

"Tomorrow we will reach the mesa country south of the village of Mancos. Now, Stone, we have it straight from a good source that you've come up on some Spanish silver and we aim to have it. I expect you to take us to it without games or delay."

"And if I don't?" No point to claim he knew nothing about the silver. It would've become common knowledge in Mancos by now. He had to find out what Wilson had in mind for him and Shanni.

James Gibson

"You'll watch Mohon carve on the little woman. Kaibito's told me about you two. You decide how it'll be."

"If I cooperate, you'll kill us anyway."

"Well, I've thought about that. I don't kill people for fun, and I just want the silver. Since you'll likely never see us again, I was inclined to let you ride out, but Kaibito's got plans for you. That's part of his reward for helping us. The way I see it, you're no worse off, it just puts you back where you were with him anyway."

"Except we were armed and had a fighting chance."

Kaibito had walked over to monitor the conversation, watching Wilson and Long. Caleb guessed that Kaibito did not understand English well and was suspicious of a trick. Wilson glanced up at Kaibito and Caleb saw that Wilson knew his plan was risky. Wilson did not like this part, but he was cool under pressure. Caleb guessed that Wilson had once been a better man. He still had some scruples.

"Can't be helped," Wilson finished. "Best I can do for you."

Caleb nodded. He had no choice but to cooperate and hope that some chance would present itself. Wilson was not bluffing; he'd let Kaibito's man torture Shanni if necessary, but Caleb had seen Wilson's distrust of Kaibito in his eyes. He knew he had to build on that.

They were climbing higher in altitude and the cold wind of autumn tugged at them, soughing through the pines to chill their breath. Shanni draped a blanket about her, holding it close to screen out the chill. Caleb donned an old poncho as they rode in silence, single file. The trail became rough with broken rockslides and talus slopes. The riders strung out, letting the horses pick their way. Caleb paused to let his horse catch its breath and Wilson pulled up alongside.

"Rough country," Wilson observed. "I'll be glad to be rid of it."

"Wilson, I don't owe you a thing, but you don't know Kaibito like I do. He's insane where whites are concerned. He'll never let you ride out of here with that silver."

Wilson considered a moment. "I'll take the warning for what it's worth, but I know Kaibito better than you think. Where do you think he's been getting his guns?"

So that's the connection, Caleb thought, nudging his horse forward. Wilson had been doing business with Kaibito, and that's why he'd seized the chance to get Caleb's help and aid Kaibito at the same time. Caleb knew he had Wilson thinking and Kaibito was already suspicious. Let the tension between them build, Caleb thought, maybe it would provide an opportunity to defend himself.

They camped at dusk in the shadow of Ute Mountain to the north. The temperature continued to drop with the setting sun and everyone clung to the warmth of the campfire. They ate in silence, each lost in his thoughts. Kaibito's eyes blazed with distrust between Caleb and Wilson, but Wilson studied his food as he ate, ignoring his surroundings. Shanni leaned against Caleb, dozing, tired from the long ride.

"Reckon we should be getting close by now," Wilson said, looking up at Caleb. "How far?"

"I haven't come this way before, but I'd guess we'll be there tomorrow afternoon."

Wilson grunted his satisfaction and Kaibito's eyes glittered, unreadable. Mohon had left after eating, probably to scout their back trail, Caleb thought. Maybe they feared trouble from the Utes who ranged the area. Wilson was becoming aware of the odds against his success, Caleb guessed. He would earn every coin he hauled out of here.

The sound of approaching horses broke the stillness. The men dismounted and Mohon appeared, pushing a prisoner in front of him.

"I found this one on our back trail," Mohon opened. "He is Oljato, one of Manuelito's scouts."

"What's he doing following us?" Wilson was looking at Kaibito as he spoke.

"He says he was left at Goulding's trading post when Porter and the troops pulled out," Mohon answered. "His orders were to find Stone and the girl."

"What do we do with him?" Wilson asked, still looking at Kaibito.

"Kill him. I'll take care of it." Kaibito drew his knife.

"Wait." Caleb spoke in the stillness, thinking fast. "I wouldn't be too hasty. If you're heading south with the silver, he's your pass through the Navaho nation."

"Tie him up for now." Wilson said. "We might need him later."

"I am Navaho." Kaibito replied angrily. "I do not need a pass through my own land!"

Wilson turned. "Does that mean you're going with us?"

Kaibito hesitated, caught off guard. His eyes blazed hatred at Caleb.

"Hold him for now if you wish," he said to Wilson. "We'll deal with him later."

Oljato sat dejected. Caleb sensed that more than met the eye was happening here. Why was Oljato on their trail alone? And Caleb doubted that Mohon could catch Oljato so easily. Caleb began to hope; maybe Oljato had brought help. He leaned over to whisper to Shanni. "I don't know what all this means, but there may be a chance for us to escape soon. Stay close and be ready."

Chapter 28

Matal was worried. Oljato should have reported back by now. Oljato had scouted ahead and confirmed that Shanni and Caleb were prisoners of Kaibito and the strangers. Since then Matal and the Huastecs had been carefully closing the gap with the riders. Oljato had rode ahead to watch Kaibito's camp and find a way to rescue Caleb and Shanni.

Matal proceeded with caution. He was not sure of the route, but he sensed they were nearing the mesa country of his home. A wrong turn would mean delay, and delay could cost the lives of Caleb and Shanni.

Matal and the Huastecs were on the move at daybreak, attempting to track Kaibito's band a half-day ahead. The trail grew difficult, winding in and out of the rough, rocky basins that separated the green-topped mesas. Matal saw that the sign of passage was disappearing on the hard rock. Soon they would be unable to track Kaibito's band.

Hours passed. Near noon the trail vanished completely. Looking ahead, Matal saw that the draw they were riding up ended in a box canyon. Sheer walls loomed on either side with no exit. They had missed the trail. They would have to turn around and go back. Matal's heart sank as he gathered the others around him and took stock. They had come close, but now they were lost. Time was running out. They had to decide what to do.

"Let's find a way to the top of the mesa," he said. "We'll ride north for Mesa Verde. Maybe we'll cut their trail."

Kaibito and the others were traversing a broad expanse of mesa when Mohon rejoined them. Caleb had seen him riding to leave a false trail in case there were others in pursuit. If pursuers got lost in these canyons, Caleb thought, it could take days to find their way out. Any help would come much too late for him and Shanni.

James Gibson

The aroma of juniper lent a tang to the cool air and brought back memories of his days at Mesa Verde. They rode past a break in the forest along the rim and far across the canyon, set in a hollow in the side of the adjoining mesa, he saw Cliff Palace, the stone dwelling that had once housed hundreds of the Ancients. Now it stood ghostlike, silent. Shanni had seen it and Caleb saw her look away, blinking back tears.

Soon it disappeared as they rode higher, climbing toward the head of the canyon. Caleb had taken his bearings from the sun and knew they would soon reach the ravine where the Spanish coins were hidden. He recalled the day that Tonah had revealed the treasure to him, explaining that Indians had attacked a mule train from silver mine to the north. The soldiers had retreated with the shipment up a long draw and managed to hide it before being overcome. Only a few of the soldiers had escaped with their lives. One, gravely wounded, had been found by the Huastecs and nursed back to health. He had stayed, married, and lived out his life in the quiet peace of Mesa Verde. He had been Shanni's great-grandfather, and the source of her Spanish blood.

They rode around the head of the canyon and swung eastward, crossing the narrow finger of the adjoining mesa. The trail approached the rim and a narrow, gravelly path that led at an angle off the rim, making a series of switchbacks to bottom. A fresh rockslide littered the dry canyon floor. Across and up a slope of broken talus, lay the hidden entrance to the cave containing the silver.

"This is it," Caleb spoke, almost to himself. He was remembering how Gillis, Inman's foreman, had tried to kill Caleb and take the silver for himself. He had been careless in his haste, and died of snakebite still clutching hands full of silver coins. Later he and Inman had faced off, and Inman had lost. How many would die due to their greed before this day ended?

Wilson and Kaibito had ridden closer, crowding Caleb's horse. Kaibito's eyes glittered as he looked down the canyon in anticipation. Wilson, too, seemed strangely agitated.

"Take this path to the canyon floor," Caleb explained. "Climb the talus slope to the narrow ledge that ends with that gnarled pine, about halfway up. The entrance to the cave is on an angle, hidden from direct view. You'll see it once you're beside the pine."

146

Wilson watched Caleb as he spoke, trying to read if he was lying. After all the effort, this part seemed almost too easy.

They rode single file down the gravel path and reached the canyon floor. Wilson left Long with the captives while he, Kaibito, and Mohon climbed up to check the cave. Caleb saw them reach the ledge and disappear into the cave. Moments passed, and then each of them reappeared carrying a pack and climbed down.

"Madre Dios!" Wilson swore as he opened the aged, cracked leather pack and silver coins spilled out. "There's a wagon load in there!"

Wilson stopped as he realized the immensity of their task. Even with all the horses loaded, not half of the treasure could be transported, and they still had to get it down out of the cave.

"I was told there were thirty mules in the train, with two packs each. I doubt one wagon would haul it," Caleb observed, watching Kaibito and Wilson.

Kaibito and Mohon were strangely quiet, hefting hands full of coins.

"Well, let's get to it," Wilson said. "It'll take the rest of the day to load the horses and get them up to camp. Untie the prisoners, we need every hand we can get."

Hours passed as they made the slow trips up and down the slope with loads of silver. Caleb stayed near Shanni, giving her a hand through the rough part of the climb. The packs were heavy, and the cracked leather, rotten with age, did not hold together well.

Wilson and Kaibito did not stop bringing the packs down until a large mound was piled beside the horses. Due to their greed, every horse was loaded. The men would have to walk.

Perspiring from exertion, the men set to loading the heavy packs. In their haste, they had not bothered to tie up Caleb and the others. Caleb knew their time grew short, but still saw no break for escape.

"That's it." Wilson turned to Kaibito. "Time to go. The rest will stay put until we return. Let's move out."

Kaibito was standing on the other side of his horse, tying a pack. Mohon had moved off a few paces. Wilson read the threat and looked at Long.

Caleb nudged Shanni out of the line of fire, behind a loaded horse.

Kaibito fired his gun as he stepped around the horse. Wilson spun, his half-drawn revolver spouting flame. His first bullet went wide, and then he steadied himself and fired. The bullet burned along Kaibito's back as Kaibito ducked under the horse and fired again. The bullet knocked Wilson off his feet to lie still.

Mohon swung his rifle, killing Long where he stood. Long fell forward, his gun unfired.

"I should've listened to you," Wilson gasped. "All that silver..." and he was gone.

One of the horses bolted, dragging its reins down the canyon. Kaibito dusted himself off and looked at Caleb and Shanni.

"Now," he said. "Time for you two. You won't be making the trip back."

He drew his knife and advanced, his smile matching the madness in his eyes.

"Stop!"

The voice rang down from the rim, followed by a hail of bullets. Mohon choked, dropping his rifle as he fell in a heap. Kaibito was knocked off his feet, and then he was rolling toward Caleb and the shooting stopped. Caleb shoved Shanni back, out of Kaibito's path, as Kaibito scrambled past Caleb and down the dry wash. He stood up to run down the canyon.

Caleb dashed for Mohon's rifle and swung it up to fire. The firing pin clicked on an empty chamber. Firing resumed from the rim of the canyon, too late, as Kaibito disappeared around a bend. Matal and the Huastecs come down the path to join them as Caleb hugged Shanni to him.

"It's over. We're safe, and Matal is here to help us get home."

They gathered up the horses and climbed out of the canyon. As they crossed the mesa, Shanni suddenly paused, looking down at the former dwelling of the Huastecs.

"Please take me to the spring, Caleb. There is something I must have when I return to my people."

Leaving Matal and the band to go on, they turned away and rode to a narrow trail that led down off the rim. They passed the former fields of the Huastecs, now lying fallow. They continued up the streambed to the scope of box elders that hid the grotto of the spring.

They dismounted and walked into the cool interior, listening to the refreshing sound of fresh water dripping into the small pool.

Water lilies lined the narrow channel carved from the rock, doomed now that the spring was dying.

Caleb could tell that something was troubling Shanni and he reached out as she lowered her head in the dim light.

"What's wrong?"

"It was here that I first knew I loved you, and you came to love me. I never knew such happiness. Now I am a different person. I have learned to hate, and I have spilled blood. I can never go back to being the woman you loved then. I cannot expect you to marry me knowing what I have done."

Caleb turned her gently and pulled her to him. "All you've done is grow up. We all have to make tough choices to survive. The part of you that I love will never change. We will go forward and deal with the world as it is, not as we wish it to be. Have no concern, I want you more than ever."

Shanni blinked back tears as she stooped to gather water lilies in a cloth and then turned to go.

THE DAY HAD been quiet in Mancos and Odie grumbled as he set about closing the mercantile. Odie's thoughts were always on money and a slow day meant little cash coming into the till. He locked the front door and, following habit, shuffled into his office to count the cash receipts. He heard a slight noise and stopped to listen. He turned back, twirled the knob on the safe, and locked in the cash. He re-entered the large room of the mercantile and moved through the shadows to lock the back door. Checking the catch, he grunted with satisfaction and turned. He froze, a scream starting in his throat as the tall Indian confronted him from the shadows, light glistening from a long knife held high. Kaibito swung viciously, ripping out Odie's vocal chords as he fell, his head half-severed from his body. There was a long, bloody gasp and he was dead.

Chapter 29

Abustle of activity surrounded the camp of the Navahos along the Chaco River. The young men brought in game and stew pots were boiling. Old men tended the deer spits roasting over open fires as women kneaded corn cakes in wooden bowls.

An air of celebration filled the camp, for it was the wedding week of Shanni and Caleb Stone. Children ran to and fro, caught up in the excitement. Freshly washed finery on makeshift clotheslines created flashes of color in the sunlight.

The wedding was to be conducted in accordance with the rituals of the Huastecs. In lieu of a kiva, Tonah, Caleb and the young men of the Huastecs were outfitting the prayer lodge of the Navaho for Caleb's sacred preparation ceremony. Afterwards, the men moved to the nearby communal lodge where in effect Caleb was celebrating his bachelor party.

Cactus wine was flowing and there was much drinking and laughter as Caleb took the good-natured ribbing of the men.

"Smoke and drink while you can, Caleb Stone!" Matal was tipsy and in great humor. "Soon you will not be able to do so in your own lodge. A wife draws circles around the home. You will have to sneak off into the woods to smoke, like a young buck who filches his father's tobacco!"

The others laughed at Caleb's expense, and Manuelito took up the theme.

"Matal is wise beyond his years. When a man loses his heart, he gains sons and daughters but gives up his freedom. Like water rubbing on a rock, he is forced to grow in character from the constant demands placed upon him."

Tonah smiled. For the first time in months he felt at peace. The Huastecs were together and welcome in Manuelito's camp for as long as they wished to stay. The trials in the desert were behind them and the young men were stronger from the experiences. They had matured quickly, learning and appreciating the immensity of the world beyond Mesa Verde.

Now they were training with Manuelito's warriors, learning to use firearms and developing the skills of seasoned fighting men. When the time came to continue the journey south, they would know what to do.

The young men, full of energy, grew bored and began to drift outside to engage in spirited games. Competition grew serious as the Huastecs and Navaho tested their strength and skill in wrestling and throwing. The Huastecs competed fiercely, but long years of survival in the desert had honed the skills of the Navaho and they were seldom bested. This made victory all the better when a Huastec managed to overcome experience with zeal.

The feasting began as the sun sank low in the west. The stews were sampled, followed by corn bread and fresh vegetables from the Navaho fields. Roast venison and wild fowl followed as the main dishes. The eating was leisurely, lasting for hours, as people ate and visited, enjoying conversation and laughter. To finish off the meal, the Navaho had prepared delicacies of pastries and wild honey, fresh berries and fruit. It was a meal fit for kings, Caleb thought, and no less deserved by the people of this great country.

Musicians brought out wooden flutes, chimes, and large hide drums to begin the music of celebration. Singers added harmonious voices, chanting prayers and good wishes for the couple that would come together as two, and go forth as one.

Caught up in the music, dancers moved in circles lit by the fires, their colorful costumes and tinkle of jewelry blending with the rhythm of the music. Tonight all would celebrate, and tomorrow Caleb Stone and Shanni would be wed.

The Huastec men hustled Caleb off to a nearby lodge to show him the clothes prepared for him to wear: tan breeches made of cotton grown by the Huastecs, richly embroidered with topstitching. Next he saw a white linen shirt embroidered with symbols of Huastec gods. A gold medallion would be worn about his neck, and gold wristlets put in place. Cotton sandals, immaculately white and unstained, completed his wardrobe. All was in order. He would join the crowd to see Shanni's march to her preparation lodge, and then he would dress for the wedding ceremony.

Multi-colored flames from bonfires lit the assembly as the people rose in silence, and separated expectantly, forming a path through the center. Caleb watched as Shanni emerged from a nearby lodge, accompanied by her attendants. She stood tall and lithe, a goddess dressed in white doeskin that outlined the curve of her body and fell gracefully to the ground. Matching leather sandals adorned her feet.

Her raven hair glistened in the firelight, held up by gold pins that matched the gold amulet and bands about her neck and wrists. A single white lily carefully preserved from the spring was placed in her hair over her left ear. She was stunningly beautiful, and Caleb felt a lump in his throat as she moved forward, surrounded by her attendants to enter her lodge to make final preparations for the ceremony.

Chapter 30

Jorge Tupac led the sentinels up the stone steps to the top of the long-abandoned Mayan temple. He touched the torch to light the ceremonial fire and then gazed over the forest to the sea shimmering in the light of the full moon. The firelight cast shadows of red and gold across their somber faces as they formed a circle, chanting softly.

Heat from the fire rose, warming them in the chill of the night as smoke drifted upward to dissipate into the night air. An aura of unreality enveloped the group and the landscape began to shimmer.

As they focused on the fire, individual perceptions melded into a group awareness that rose upward on the smoke and hovered over the complex of stone temples. The ghosts of former inhabitants crowded the plaza, frozen in time as a reminder of the past energy of the sentinels. A giant figure, cast crimson by the firelight, began forming out of the void, hovering over them so that Jorge and the sentinels looked up as one, "seeing" the figure outlined in robes and shadows.

"Now is the time," it said. "The nodes of the matrix in the land of your enemies has shifted in your favor. There is a mortal whose hatred drives him with all-consuming intensity to kill your enemies. You must add your strength and channel him to assure success while the probabilities are favorable."

"How will we know this one?" Jorge asked.

"Follow the matrix. You will find him where his hatred deforms the energy field."

"What of Tonah, the sorcerer? Twice he has thwarted us using the ancient powers."

"Focus on the woman, Shanni. Her death will destroy the will of Tonah, and that of the potential sorcerer known as Stone. As long as the woman lives, they are strong."

"I requested assistance. Our enemies utilize great strength against us."

"The sentinels will provide support, but you must channel their resources. You spend too much energy equivocating. You have the responsibility and you must seize the power. If you fail, you will die."

The figure began to fade as Jorge choked down his fear, searching for words to hold the apparition, but it had disappeared back into the void.

Jorge's awareness returned to the fire. The sentinels stood silently, staring at him. They had perceived his instructions. They would support but he must lead.

Terror drove him as he looked to the north and launched his perilous journey.

CALEB HAD RETURNED to his lodge to dress when Shanni's shrill scream rang across the settlement. He rushed toward Shanni's lodge as he saw Kaibito, knife in hand, struggling to climb out of the tear he had made in her tent. Caleb reacted instinctively, leaping onto Kaibito, driving him clear of the lodge and back into the shadows.

Caleb fought desperately to keep control of Kaibito's knife hand as they rolled in the dust. Kaibito swung viciously, narrowly missing Caleb as he rolled away. Rage surged in Caleb as he gained his feet and hammered heavy blows into Kaibito, driving him backward. The knife slipped from Kaibito's grasp, and he broke free to race away in the direction of the river.

As his eyes adjusted to the dim light, Caleb grasped the dropped knife and ran after Kaibito's fleeing form. Kaibito splashed across the shallow stream and grasped frantically for his horse. Kaibito swung into the saddle as Caleb leaped up behind and fought to hold on as the terrified horse bolted into the river.

Kaibito twisted and drove Caleb's knife hand down to slice along Caleb's arm. Caleb felt the arm go numb as fresh blood welled up on his tunic. In desperation, Caleb jerked the knife upward and felt the point go in deep under Kaibito's left arm.

Kaibito screamed and pulled away, causing Caleb to lose his balance and drag Kaibito with him as he fell from the plunging horse.

Caleb staggered to his knees as Kaibito unleashed a vicious kick to the head, knocking him over. Kaibito seemed to have superhuman power, Caleb thought, in a bloody haze. Nothing he did broke Kaibito's attack.

Kaibito gouged at Caleb's eyes as Caleb's hand closed on a rock. Caleb brought the rock up hard along Kaibito's temple. Blood spurted but Kaibito became stronger, more savage. Caleb felt delirious, his head swimming from the beating and loss of blood. He thought he saw the faint forms of ghosts in the darkness, pumping energy into Kaibito's body. Caleb felt weariness overcoming him, and knew he must act or die. A primordial rage rose from deep within his being, the last reserves of an organism fighting for its life.

He would never accept death at the hands of this madman. He was beyond thinking, beyond feeling, his entire being focused on one point, to kill Kaibito, to rend him, to forever eliminate his as a threat to Shanni. Caleb reached out and seized Kaibito by the throat. Kaibito thrashed, beating at Caleb trying to break his hold, but Caleb was beyond caring.

"Damn you!" Caleb screamed. "For Shanni!"

Wild fear crossed Kaibito's bloody face as Caleb choked down on his windpipe and twisted, bringing the full weight of his body to bear. Kaibito's neck broke with a sharp snap and his body went slack, his eyes glazing in the dim light.

Caleb's rage turned to the evil beings that had helped Kaibito. He launched his awareness outward, riding the white-hot beam of his anger as it reached toward them. They had withdrawn the energy from Kaibito and encased themselves in its protection. Psychic energy dueled and flashed as Caleb's rage met their combined resistance.

"Not yet," Caleb felt Tonah's voice in his mind. "Remember, but now see to Shanni."

Realization hit Caleb like a bullet, and he felt his delirium clear. Shanni! Was she alive? He must go to her!

He came to his senses standing over Kaibito's lifeless body. He was shaking, his tunic soaked with blood.

Manuelito came to him and directed his steps as he staggered back toward camp. A surgeon from Porter's troop had arrived at the lodge and set about tending Shanni's wound. Blood soaked her body and the furs that lined the floor. Caleb knelt down to hold her hand, but she was lifeless, barely breathing.

"Come," Manuelito said. "We must let the physician do his work. Let's see to your wounds."

Caleb was too weak to resist and allowed himself to be led to a nearby lodge where the Huastecs bandaged his wounds.

"I'll be all right," Caleb said as the strength went out of him. "Just let me rest a little while."

It seemed only a few moments had passed when he awakened with a gnawing thirst and drank from the canteen set by his bed.

Manuelito was seated nearby and rose when he saw Caleb had awakened.

"Shanni?" Caleb whispered.

"The little princess breathes but she sleeps and does not awaken. The surgeon of the pony soldiers is with her."

"How long?"

"We brought you here this morning. It is now evening."

"Good lord! I've got to go to her!"

Manuelito helped him get up and walk to the wedding lodge.

The surgeon was tending a cold compress on Shanni's forehead while Tonah sat quietly nearby. Tonah's face was strained, his eyes deep-set with worry. Caleb looked at Shanni's ashen face. Deep blue circles outlined her eyes and only the slight movement of her chest revealed that she was alive.

Caleb turned to the surgeon in silent appeal.

"I don't know what to tell you," the surgeon said. "She lost some blood, but not enough to be life-threatening. Somehow she's slipped into a coma. All we can do now is wait and pray. If she awakens, she should be all right."

Caleb was wracked with grief and worry. To know happiness and risk having it taken away was more than he could bear.

"Please come with me," Tonah said quietly. Caleb followed as he walked outside and led to the edge of the river.

Shanni struggled weakly as she looked up at the foreboding statue lit by the crystal. Her body was suspended in a cocoon of light that slowly tightened, constricting her breathing. She could not scream and she could not break free. She moved her eyes to gaze down at the man who smiled evilly as he directed the energy beam from the crystal to the statue, and then to her cocoon. Who was he? And why was he slowly killing her? She tried to use her powers to break free, but she was too weak; she could not overcome the energy arrayed against her. She needed Caleb. She needed to envelop herself in his strength! Waves of sadness and grief washed over her as she realized she was losing him. She was dying and they would be separated forever. The energy field adjusted, feeding off of her grief, and she realized her emotions were being used against her.

A strange peace seeped into the cocoon. She floated gently, released from her worries and cares. She was crossing over into death and it felt so peaceful. What was there to fear?

"Watch. Watch and remember."

The memory of Tonah's words shocked her and she instinctively pulled back. What was she thinking? She was giving in to death! She had been here before and had returned to her world. She remembered that she had been an observer, neutralizing her feelings.

Instinctively she dismissed desire and worry from her mind. She calmed and centered herself as she remembered Tonah's words. She would wait for Tonah to find her and show her the way back home.

In the light of the crystal, Jorge cursed and increased the energy field. Success had almost been within his grasp.

TONAH STOPPED BESIDE the shallow water of the Chaco River and turned to Caleb.

"Shanni is in the grip of evil forces. Without help she will die. I am not strong enough to defeat them alone. The time has come for you to decide."

Caleb felt a chill run through him. "What do you mean?"

"There are supernatural forces that we must combat to save Shanni's life. I need you to go with me to confront these forces, but to do so you must believe they are real."

"I could say I believe, but what if I really don't"

"At best, we may not prevail and Shanni will die. At worst, we could all die."

Caleb filled with dread as he stared unseeing at the water. What was he to do? Could the son of John Elias Stone embrace sorcery and witchcraft? He would do anything to save Shanni, but could he go against the values he had carried all his life?

Tonah understood Caleb's torment. A person could lie to others, but there was only the truth when a person confronted himself.

"Remember the struggle with Kaibito. That will help. You saw the beings that were arrayed against you."

"I thought I was delirious, hallucinating."

"Your mind had to construct something to explain the unexplainable. If you can accept the possibility that what happened was real, then we can proceed."

"And if I cannot?"

"Then there is faith."

"I don't understand."

"There are times when we trust to faith, although it is not real in the sense of being tangible. You will have to suspend disbelief and have faith. You must act, following your feelings and accepting what will be."

"I'll do anything for Shanni."

"Then please go to the water, reach down below the surface and select a small stone that you can hold in your left hand. Sense the coolness and wetness of the water, and the smoothness of the stone in your hand. Then come back and sit down by me."

Caleb fought his sense of losing control. Shanni was dying and he was picking stones from the river. It was madness! But he complied. What else could he do? He picked the stone as directed, and returned with it dripping water.

"Please sit down, close your eyes, breath deeply and follow me."

Caleb's heart was pounding as he sat down next to Tonah and breathed, trying to calm his agitated feelings. He felt like he was losing his mind, sitting here with Tonah when he should be with Shanni. Doubts began bubbling up, and his breath came in short gasps. He felt the stone drying and growing warm in his hand.

"Listen to the water," Tonah said. "Listen to the river. Try to follow it."

Caleb focused on the sound of the water and his breathing slowed. He felt a quietness settle over him and a sense of acceptance. A feeling of trust and well-being came over him, and he accepted the sense of being a natural part of the universe.

"Good." He felt Tonah's voice, but somehow he knew Tonah had not spoken. "Now we can proceed. I'll coach you as we go. It is essential that you do not react to your feelings, or you will pull away and become lost. Let whatever you feel, terror, horror, or seduction roll over you like the water of the river. Do not let it cling to you. Trust yourself and follow me."

Caleb felt his awareness flicker, as if the world was shaking ever so slightly, and felt himself floating upward. Tonah appeared beside him and reached out to grasp his shoulder. Pitch-blackness enveloped them and Caleb felt his stomach roll, as if they were falling headlong through an abyss. They were out of control and he felt terror welling up in him.

"Remember to let go. Don't let the emotions cling. Trust yourself." Tonah's voice coached out of the blackness.

With an effort, Caleb calmed himself and the sensation of falling faded.

"I would have a Guide," Tonah commanded into the void.

The blackness wavered and Caleb saw a robed and hooded figure outlined in the darkness. He could not make out the features. The figure reminded him of pictures of the Grim Reaper he'd seen as a child, and he recoiled reflexively.

"Steady," he felt Tonah's voice in his ear.

As he gained experience, Caleb realized what Tonah had been trying to tell him. He must detach himself from his feelings. No matter what happened, he must control his emotions and simply observe. He would no longer embrace fear for "himself."

"What do you wish?" The apparition said.

"A guidepost for our return."

"So be it."

A beacon of light began to form out of the blackness, and it cast light upon a tranquil scene that looked vaguely familiar. Caleb realized it was a bird's-eye view of Manuelito's village. As the light brightened, the apparition disappeared back into the void. A second beacon split off from the first and extended outward, as far as Caleb could see.

"Follow me," Tonah's voice said. "Extend your awareness and ride on the beam of light."

Caleb felt momentarily unsettled. He didn't know how to follow Tonah's instructions. Uncertainty began to creep into his mind.

"Stop! You must trust. Let go and follow me!"

Caleb felt a sensation of acceleration as the light engulfed them, and then it stopped. He had the disconcerting feeling of being "everywhere" at once.

He felt Tonah's hand on his shoulder and his surroundings glimmered. He was standing in a dark room with stone walls. The stench of death reached his nostrils and he started to recoil, but then he caught himself and let it wash over him. A bright beam of energy traveled from a glass-like stone to illuminate a statue, and then to a cocoon of energy that slowly rotated, giving off flashes of multi-colored light. As his eyes adjusted, he recognized Shanni's quiet form, lying deathlike inside the cocoon.

He felt a surge of emotion, but he was learning. With an effort, he forced himself to stay calm.

"Good." Tonah said. "Now concentrate on the beam of light. Together we will bend it from the cocoon to focus on the evil little man standing by the crystal."

Jorge felt their intent and called upon the guardian. Out of the shadows, a personification of evil began to emerge. The being glistened like onyx as it added a blue-white beam of pure energy reinforcing the crystal. Tonah gasped and staggered back as the intensified light beam enveloped his body.

"Now, Caleb!" Tonah's voice screamed in Caleb's brain. "It's up to you! If they succeed, Shanni dies!"

Tonah's words struck at Caleb's heart, breaking his composure. He cast about wildly; what was he supposed to do? In the midst of turmoil, he suddenly found the quiet place of his center, and felt his emotions focusing into a single resolve. Life and death ceased to have meaning; he was in another place, and he knew he would never let these evil beings take Shanni.

Without conscious effort, he felt his hands lift and he was holding the beam of energy as it pulsed between his hands. His hands attempted to channel the energy and it enveloped him in a blazing flash, thrusting him backwards. He steadied himself and began to channel the energy in a great arc away from Shanni's cocoon and back toward Jorge and the guardian. He heard Jorge screaming as the blue-white blaze began to consume him and the guardian. With a blinding flash, Jorge and the guardian disappeared as the smell of ozone permeated the air.

Caleb turned to Shanni as the cocoon around her began to dissolve. A great sense of relief and joy swept through him.

"Not yet!" Tonah warned. "It's a trap!"

Just in time Caleb realized that other sentinels, unseen in the shadows, had been waiting for him to succumb to emotion. The beings reactivated the energy beam, but now Caleb filled with a terrible resolve, and he knew what to do.

He focused his will to bending the beam, and watched grimly as the energy engulfed the sentinels, outlining them like skeletons as it disintegrated their bodies. Caleb heard their shrieks as the beam disintegrated in an explosion that shook the stone chamber.

"Quickly!" Tonah's voice commanded. "We must take Shanni home!"

Tonah reached out and placed his hand on Shanni's shoulder. She looked tired and bewildered, but she was alive.

"Tonah, I knew you'd find me."

She turned, reaching out to Caleb.

"Not yet! No emotion!" Tonah cut in. "Follow me."

Tonah stretched his hands toward the beacon light and Caleb again felt a sense of movement. Caleb looked down and saw the familiar village of the Navaho. Tonah led, holding onto Shanni, as the beacon disappeared and they were lost in the blackness of the void.

A sense of disorientation overcame Caleb as he lost sight of Tonah and Shanni. He felt as if he were falling out of control.

And then he saw the glade. He was twelve again, and Becky Sims, his first love was beckoning him to the quiet spot behind the schoolhouse. She was filling out in the fullness of womanhood and he had loved her from afar. In his adolescent desire, he had wanted her but had lacked the confidence to pursue her. One day she had hugged him playfully, flattered by his interest, but she had been older and soon married and moved away, leaving him unfulfilled. He had forgotten his sense of loss all these years, but now he could get a second chance. She was beckoning him, calling him to fulfill his longing and complete his desire. At long last he could have her.

"Focus on the stone," Tonah's voice came to him faintly, as if in a dream. "Listen for the river."

Caleb didn't want to hear; he tried to ignore the voice. He wanted only to be young again and to be with Becky. But a worry nagged at the core of his being; he could not ignore the memory of the stone, cold and wet in his hand. Sudden realization hit him: as Tonah had warned, he was being seduced to his doom by his emotions! Until now he had not understood.

Caleb recoiled and the scene disappeared, thrusting him back into darkness and disorientation. He remembered the signpost and looked about frantically, wanting desperately to regain control and stop the feeling of falling. In the void a bird's-eye view of the river began to appear.

Caleb felt a vibration, and a wave of nausea, as the earth seemed to move and then steady itself. He heard the familiar sound of the water and slowly opened his eyes to view the river.

He was drenched in perspiration, and burning with thirst. He staggered to the river and dipped his head under the water, savoring its coolness. He raised his head to drink deeply, and wiped his mouth with his hand. He was exhausted, hardly able to rise as he turned to look at Tonah, seated nearby. Had it all been a dream? Or a nightmare?

Tonah opened his eyes and sighed. "It is done. Now let us go to Shanni."

They entered the lodge and Caleb moved to Shanni's side, clasping her hand.

She stirred, let out a long sigh and opened her eyes. "Many children," she whispered. "We shall have many children, Caleb," and she smiled.

RAMON PIMA LED HIS heavily laden burro down the dusty street to the open-air *mercado* of the village. Today, as every Saturday for many years he would sell potatoes and vegetables from his garden and catch up on the news. He would visit with friends, perhaps play a game of cards and sip a little tequila. Market day was a welcome respite from the monotony of a poor man's week.

He approached the stall of his old friend Juan, purveyor of leather goods. Juan greeted Ramon with a toothless grin and waved him over.

"Have you heard the news about Jorge?" Juan liked to be first with the latest information and over the years he had become something of an informal "town crier" for the region.

"No, tell me!" Ramon responded. He knew that Juan would tell him anyway, but why not play to his old friend's sense of importance?

"Jorge the peddler is dead. They found his body by the ruins of the old pyramid near the mountains. His body was blackened and charred. It is believed that he was struck by lightning!"

"How strange!" Ramon shook his head. "I saw him only days ago and he appeared ill. He told me that he had been touched by lightning. What are the chances that he would be struck again by lightning?"

Juan paused, scratching his head. "That is more news! Wait until people hear that he was chased by the lightning until it caused his death!"

Juan hurried off to spread the latest insight into the death of Jorge Tupac the peddler.

Ramon crossed himself, invoking divine protection from long habit from evil he did not understand, and continued with his burro down the street.

IT WAS EARLY morning when Caleb finished his breakfast and wandered casually along the quiet stream that was the Chaco River. He had been unsettled since participating in Tonah's sorcery to save Shanni. He experienced recurring headaches and restless nights filled with vivid dreams. He wondered if he was becoming mentally unbalanced.

He looked up and saw Tonah sitting quietly in the shade of the cottonwoods. As Caleb approached he saw that Tonah's eyes were closed as if he were napping.

"Good morning, Caleb," Tonah greeted without opening his eyes. "I've been expecting you."

Caleb felt a wave of discomfort in his stomach and his nerves tingled. Why was he having a physical reaction to Tonah's voice?

"I don't understand," Caleb responded, pausing. "I was just wandering about, preoccupied."

"I know. You did not consciously set out to come here, but sometimes one's body knows where to go to seek healing. You have been unbalanced since Kaibito's attack. Like a flower that turns its face to the sun, your body seeks a source of balance and centeredness."

"Does it show? My being unsettled, I mean. I thought I was just feeling out of sorts and not sleeping well. I used a lot of energy against Kaibito. He had superhuman strength and fought like a madman. He almost killed me."

"That's part of it. Your body took a beating, but food and sleep will overcome that. Your energy drain is now centered in your mind. That is why you cannot sleep restfully."

Caleb found himself sitting down, unbidden, next to Tonah.

Tonah opened his eyes. "Take a moment to focus. Remain silent and look at the water. Hear its murmur. Feel the breeze. Let the serenity of this place at this moment of time calm you. After you calm yourself, close your eyes and continue to experience this place as if your eyes were open, for in a sense they will be."

Caleb felt his pulse rate rising as looking at the water triggered his memory of the shamanistic journey to rescue Shanni. He recoiled as his body remembered the fear and uncertainty, the feeling of losing control.

"Let go of those feelings," Tonah's voice interrupted. "Let them flow over you like water. Do not cling to them. Simply accept that you are here, safe and at peace. This is your life at this moment. You are part of creation, and it is a part of you. You are inseparable from it."

Caleb found Tonah's words confusing, but he discarded them as he discarded the feeling of fear. He took a long breath and let it out slowly. He did not have to understand, he had only to accept. His pulse slowed and he felt serene yet highly-alert. His mind stilled and he was content as the murmur of the water soothed him. A feeling of well being filled him as he appreciated the beauty of the moment.

"That's better," Tonah said softly. "Now that you are centered, we can deal with the sources of your conflict. You can express what you have been experiencing."

Caleb felt thoughts returning, and realized for a moment his mind had been quiet, not thinking, just experiencing. Intuitively he resisted returning, for with his thoughts came agitation. How could he relate his thoughts without offending Tonah?

As if in response to his turmoil, Tonah began speaking. "From the time we are little children, we learn to build walls around our feelings. We learn what to express to receive love and affection, and what to hide to avoid pain and rejection. This becomes a key condition of survival, and our core being which I'll refer to as the 'Self', internalizes these learned responses so deeply that we lose awareness of the process.

"But this internalized response is always there, waiting to flare up when we are confronted with anything that does not fit our view of the world. The stranger the phenomenon, the more threatening it is to our world view, so our awareness attempts to anchor us in the past. To the Self, what has helped us survive in the past validates that past reality as 'truth'.

"But there comes a time when we are confronted with a reality that is contrary to the world of our past. When that happens, a crisis is created that our Self must face and resolve, or lapse into denial and neurosis.

"You are at that time and place. I invite you to discuss what you are feeling so that we may deal with it and climb to the next level of understanding."

"This is madness!" Caleb blurted out. "How can I possibly discuss it?"

"That's precisely the point, and you're making a good start. If your internal conflict were not turning your world upside down, there would be no crisis!"

Caleb's frustration turned to anger. He fought the impulse to get up and walk away. He took a deep breath to regain control.

"Stop equivocating! Be candid with me!" Tonah's voice lashed out like a slap across the face.

Rage leapt in Caleb. Who did Tonah think he was talking to? Caleb wasn't a child to be scolded at his father's knee!

"Look, with all due respect, Tonah..."

"That's my point," Tonah interrupted. "It's not 'due respect'. True friendship comes from expressing yourself, your true self. Anything less is patronizing me."

Caleb was stunned, brought up short as Tonah's point hit home. Tonah was right. As an Anglo, he had arrogantly assumed that he knew the "real world" and had all the answers. He had felt the Huastecs were naïve and that he must "save" them from the outside world. Although he had not been aware of it, he'd never met them as equals. He flushed with embarrassment.

"You're right," Caleb admitted. "Due to my gratitude to you and Shanni for saving my life, I've avoided expressing my true feelings for fear of offending you."

"That's better. First comes understanding and then comes respect. Only then is there a basis for true friendship. Now you are faced with a choice: To open up, or to draw back. To be honest with me you must be honest with yourself. We could debate which is more difficult!"

Caleb let out a long breath. "All right, at the risk of offending you, I am very uncomfortable with your shamanism. I cannot go along with casting spells, witchcraft, and such. I believe it is wrong and dangerous."

"Good. We have some mutual respect and trust or you would not be able to say that. You think I am a little mad, perhaps?"

"I know you sincerely believe in your practices, but I don't, and now it's causing me hallucinations."

"Why are you so sure? Is there no possibility my world view might be real?"

"No. I was warned against what you're doing by my father."

"What did he tell you?"

"He told us all...he was a preacher and he told all of us in the congregation that the Bible warned against detestable practices such as divination, sorcery, and witchcraft. He warned us to never listen to people who did these things, that they would lead us astray. And in my experience out in the world, he was right!"

Tonah interjected. "Yet some of your most revered religious leaders were referred to as 'seers' and asked by kings to predict the future!"

Caleb looked at Tonah, unbelieving. "Like who?' he asked.

"As I recall, the Old Testament of your religious book, the Bible, relates that Eleazar, a priest, utilized a device called the 'Urim and Thummin' to render religious decisions, and the great prophet Samuel, when asked by the future king Saul if he was the 'seer', acknowledged that he was. Numerous other prophets spoke directly with God and foretold the future."

"How could you possibly know that?"

"No shamanism involved," Tonah chuckled. "Shanni's ancestor, the Spanish soldier I told you about, carried a Bible. Once I learned Spanish, it was a simple matter to read it."

Caleb didn't know what to say. This all seemed unreal. Here he sat in a camp of the Navaho, discussing the Bible with a Huastec shaman. His senses reeled. How he would like to be back on his land, building his herd and discussing the day's activities around the campfire. That was the world he knew. If a man didn't stay focused, the world became too confusing!

"So you see," Tonah continued, "Good and evil are interpretations applied to phenomena. Your father was right to warn you against evildoers. Charlatans have led many astray. But your Self understood only a partial interpretation. Being a child, you were not able to make an informed choice. Instead, you internalized what you were told as an absolute, which precluded the possibility these practices might be used for beneficial purposes, or in other words, for 'good'. Are you now beginning to accept the possibility?"

Realization was dawning in Caleb. He had believed so strongly that he had not questioned. How many other things might he believe that precluded his awareness of truth? How could he know anything for certain?

"Let's just say I am less certain. I still think I should be taking some action, rather than sitting here. We live in the physical world, a world that's real to me. I've learned how to survive in it, and I know from grim experience it is where we live or die."

"We are predisposed to physical action when we are born," Tonah replied. "It is necessary to our survival. But we humans exist in both physical and spiritual worlds. We unwittingly use action to keep ourselves from thinking about the greater reality. By focusing on what's in front of us, we don't have to deal with all the other possibilities. Do you still think you were hallucinating when we rescued Shanni?"

"I have to think that. It could not possibly have been real. We never left the river bank!"

"Then how was it that Shanni awakened from the coma?"

Caleb recalled his feelings of fear and dread as he knelt by Shanni, her face pale and lifeless. The physician had voiced his mystification and helplessness; he'd done all he could and waited for her to live or die. Shanni's life had hung in the balance.

"What we did might have made a difference," he said. Now he could at least accept the possibility.

Tonah nodded. "You've reached a critical juncture. You can truly accept the possibility, without misleading yourself or me. This is in line with your strong sense of integrity."

"What do you mean?"

"You have been targeted for death by the sorcerers who oppose us. Already they have moved against you, attempting to take your life."

"Why me? I'd think I'd be the last person for them to be concerned with, when I don't even believe in sorcery."

"Because of your inner strength. You have strong beliefs and deep convictions. You cannot say you believe what you truly do not, and nothing outside yourself can change what you believe. That creates the potential for terrible resolve.

"Your inner strength is also the reason we had to bring about the conditions for you to face and re-examine your core beliefs against shamanism. Until you yourself accepted the possibility, nothing could change you.

" The evil sorcerers see the potential for you to become a tremendous force against them, and seek to eliminate you as a threat before you are even aware of that potential."

"No offense, but this is even more bizarre," Caleb said, shaking his head. "They wanted to eliminate me as a sorcery threat before I believed any of this was more than hallucinations?"

"You could put it that way."

"So where does this leave us?"

"I must begin your training in sorcery. I am growing old and my strength is waning. We must move quickly. Your greatest contribution to the survival of the Huastecs may well be your powers of sorcery, not your guns."

"Even though I don't believe any of this is real?"

"At least now you do not disbelieve. You can accept the possibility. That is enough for us to begin."

Tonah rose and led the way back to Manuelito's camp. Shanni was recovering her strength, sitting outside her lodge to enjoy the sun. Tonah greeted her as he and Caleb sat down beside her. The pallor in her face was gone and her eyes were bright. Caleb thought she was never more beautiful as he grasped her hand.

"I see you two have been plotting," she smiled. "Any breakthroughs?"

"He is a stubborn one," Tonah replied, smiling.

"As I warned you!" Shanni returned.

Caleb felt a surge of indignation. Did Shanni know what Tonah was up to?

"Some friends," he said. "I feel like I'm being manipulated."

Shanni turned serious. "No, my darling, our love for you forces us to make you see what we are up against. In a way, you agreed to help us without knowing what you were in for. In fairness, we did not know ourselves all the forces that would come to be arrayed against us."

"And now we must make new choices and a new commitment based on new realities," Tonah added.

"I'm starting to see," Caleb said. "Kaibito was only the beginning. Others will be sent against us. The battle has only begun."

"Precisely," Tonah agreed.

"And our wedding?" Caleb looked at Shanni.

"Should be postponed," Shanni answered. "Kaibito thought you would be with me. It was you he sought to kill. He attacked me in frustration."

"You never signed up for what we face," Tonah interjected. "You can leave with honor and return to your land and your world."

"Without Shanni?"

"If I go with you now," Shanni continued, "The the evil ones will follow. They will not allow us to live knowing that they exist. But if this is your decision, I will go with you."

"And if I stay?"

"We train hard," Shanni replied. "I will learn to use the weapons of your world; horses, knives, guns. You, if you choose to stay, will learn the weapons of our world, the tools of shamanism and sorcery."

169

"And know," Tonah added, "that the journey of the Huastecs remains perilous. Our lives will be in constant danger. Your risk will lessen if you return home."

"I have no home without Shanni. I will not return until we can go together."

Shanni took both his hands in hers. "I want nothing more than to be your wife. But we must be able to live in peace. We will hold on to our dream and make it come true."

"I still can't believe it has come to this," Caleb said, shaking his head. "I just wanted to marry Shanni and build a ranch. Now I'm becoming someone I don't know and it concerns me."

"No one seeks Power," Tonah said. "It chooses you, and thrusts itself upon you. Then you must accept, however reluctantly, without knowing where it will take you. Such is the mystery of life. Somehow your fate is entwined with that of the Huastecs."

Caleb stood up and took Shanni in his arms. He gazed across the river to the mountains lining the horizon to the south.

"Let us begin," he said.

THE END

Coming Soon:

A NASAZI QUEST, third in the ANASAZI PRINCESS series, continues the saga of the Huastecs. As Caleb Stone, Shanni and the Huastecs journey south to find their ancient homeland, they leave the United States and enter the country of Mexico during the chaotic times of its revolution. To the Huastecs, theirs is a journey of survival; to the rurales, they are an invading force. Caleb and Shanni are forced to battle the evil forces arrayed against them while struggling to find personal happiness amid the changes affecting their world.

THE FOLLOWING PAGES are a preview of this next novel in the *Anasazi Princess* series.

Prologue

Tonah, the Huastec shaman and spiritual leader of the Huastecs, approached the lodge of Shanni, his granddaughter. Shanni had reached young womanhood when circumstances forced the Huastecs to leave their home in the hidden canyons of Mesa Verde. The Huastecs found refuge with the Navaho while Shanni recovered from her attack by the renegade, Kaibito. Tonah welcomed the respite offered by the hospitality of the Navaho leader, Manuelito.

Shanni was sitting quietly in the morning sun, gazing across the Navaho camp.

"Good morning, Granddaughter," Tonah greeted. "It is good to see you up and around. You are recovering rapidly."

"Hello. Yes, I'm feeling much better and growing impatient to get on with my duties."

"And what might they be?"

"I intend to train with the Huastec men, learning the fighting skills that Manuelito's fighters will be teaching our warriors."

"That is quite an undertaking. Are you sure you will be strong enough?"

"The training will help me to recover my strength. Eventually I will be as strong as the men."

"As you wish, but it will certainly be a change of custom. You must find a way to get the men to accept you in that role."

"I know, and I've been thinking about how to do it. They will be more receptive when they realize the need. There are too few of us Huastecs to waste even one warrior, whether man or woman."

"Will it interfere with your Gift?"

"No. In fact I believe it will make it stronger. Already I am able to steady my ability to see the probabilities in the future, and I'm hopeful it will help me to look farther out to avoid danger for our people."

"That is good," Tonah agreed.

"We are so early into our journey, and already we have faced near-disaster."

"But maybe to a good purpose," Shanni interjected. "Now all of our people have a better understanding of the obstacles we face."

"They know of the physical obstacles, but they do not yet know of the evil forces arrayed against us in the spirit world. These we must fight alone."

" 'We?' Must you and I alone face the evil ones?"

"I believe that Power has given us a new and powerful ally in Caleb Stone."

"Do you think you can train him in the art of sorcery?"

"Yes. He has at least suspended disbelief, although he has a strong will and we have little time in which to train."

"Maybe even less time than we thought," Shanni interjected. "My prescience is warning that our time here is growing short. Some threat is moving toward us in the physical world, forcing us to act."

Tonah looked away with misgiving. Shanni's gift was never wrong. Something ominous was about to happen and there was little time to prepare.

Chapter 1

Caleb looked out across the Chaco River at the dust thrown up by approaching riders. Manuelito heard the hoof beats and came out of his tent to watch. As they drew closer, Caleb recognized Lieutenant Porter at the head of a squad of soldiers. Porter had become a friend to the Navaho and the Huastecs during their recent troubles with the renegade Kaibito and his band. Porter halted and dismounted near the river. He strode forward while his men watered the horses.

"Howdy," Porter said, extending a hand to Caleb, and nodding to Manuelito. "Heard you were preparing to continue your journey."

"We plan to accept Manuelito's hospitality a few more weeks while we train the Huastec men to use rifles, and Manuelito's men will teach them hand-to-hand combat skills. When they're ready, we'll move on."

"Ahuh. Well, that's why I'm here. Being peaceful, the Huastecs aren't a problem for the military. I'm happy to leave things as they are. But we've got a new Indian Agent coming in, and he's already sent word that he'll be visiting all the tribes and making a census. If you're here, he'll count the Huastecs and you won't be able to leave."

Caleb glanced at Manuelito. Porter was being a friend, letting them know, but this was bad news for the Huastecs. They'd have to face the wasteland to the south in haste and unprepared.

"How much time do we have?" Caleb asked.

"He's due by the end of the week, and sounds like he wants to get started pronto. I'd say he'll need another week to get settled, and then he'll be riding out with his escort, which'll likely be my troopers."

"We're obliged to you for giving us some warning. I'll have to discuss this with Tonah and the others, see what we can do."

"Least I could do after all we went through together fighting Kaibito."

Porter turned and walked back to rejoin his troops. With a wave he mounted and they spurred their horses across the Chaco River.

Caleb turned to Manuelito. "There are more than two hundred of the Huastecs, and we have less than two weeks. I'd better tell Tonah and the others."

Manuelito nodded his assent as Caleb hurried across the compound to find Tonah.

Tonah was sitting with Shanni outside her lodge. Shanni was regaining her strength from the attack by Kaibito that had nearly taken her life.

Tonah sensed Caleb's agitation and rose to meet him.

"I'm afraid I have bad news," Caleb said. "Lieutenant Porter stopped by to warn us that a new Indian Agent is arriving within a week. He proposed to conduct a census as soon as he arrives. If the Huastecs are still in camp, they will be counted and kept on the reservation. If you leave to complete your journey, you will be hunted down by the soldiers."

Tonah turned to Shanni. "This is grave news. We have little time to prepare."

Shanni stood up. Determination burned in her eyes as she spoke. "We must discuss this development with Matal and the others, and find a course of action. We cannot be trapped here. Our journey has just begun!"

Tonah nodded his assent. "Caleb, could I ask you to seek out Matal and give him this news. Ask him to spread the word to the other warriors, and meet tonight in my lodge. We must develop a course of action quickly to avoid panic among our people."

Caleb nodded and walked among the tents scattered along the river, looking for Matal.

The flames from torches lighted the way for the warriors assembling in Tonah's lodge. Matal and more than a dozen of the Huastec warriors gathered with Manuelito, Shanni, and Caleb as Tonah opened the meeting.

"You all have heard the news. We are grateful for the hospitality of the Navaho, and thought we had enough time to train in the skills needed to defend ourselves when we resume our journey to the Center. Now we find that time is running out. All the Huastecs must leave or we will become prisoners of the Anglo government. But we know from experience that we are not prepared to survive in the hostile country through which we must travel. This meeting is to discuss a course of action."

Matal rose to speak. "We have discussed this among ourselves," he waved a hand to include the other Huastec warriors. "We have enough silver to buy repeating rifles and revolvers. We must purchase them soon, and learn how to use them. Manuelito's warriors can teach us all the skills we need to survive the journey, but we must have time to train."

"Time is what we do not have," Tonah replied.

"Unless you can find a temporary refuge," Manuelito broke in quietly.

Matal caught the concept quickly, and turned to Manuelito. "Yes, that would buy us the time we need. What do you have in mind?"

"Kaibito's camp."

Caleb looked at Tonah for reaction, but Tonah held his peace. The Huastecs had suffered in the desert. They would fear leaving the security of Manuelito's camp and returning to a journey into the unknown. Commitment to the chosen course of action would require the consensus of the people. If the Huastec warriors agreed, the people would follow them.

Matal frowned, reviewing the suggestion. "It's big enough, and has water, but there is no source of food."

"It is isolated," Manuelito continued. "The Indian Agent would have no knowledge of it since there is no permanent settlement there. Wild game, mostly deer, is available two days' ride to the west, near Betatakin. I'd estimate a large group like the Huastecs could live there one, maybe two months before the game was depleted."

"Alternatives?" Tonah interjected.

Shanni spoke up. "We cannot return to Mesa Verde, and now we cannot stay here. We agree we are unprepared to resume our journey. I suggest we pack in supplies to the camp and supplement them with game. This will extend our stay and offset our dependence on hunting for our food."

"I agree," Caleb added. "But the more supplies we try to carry with us, the greater the need for horses and carts. With over two hundred people to move and care for, it will be difficult to travel without discovery."

"My trackers can help," Manuelito said. "They know the route, and can guide your travel. I suggest that the caravan travel at night, and hold up in hidden spots during the day. You should be able to reach the camp in five days."

Matal nodded. "It sounds like we have the beginning of a plan. Now we'll need to work out the details."

"But first we must bring all the others into the discussion," Tonah interjected. "We must get their suggestions and address their concerns. We will need the commitment of everyone for the hardships ahead."

"Well spoken," Manuelito agreed. "People will resist if they feel you are already committed to this course of action."

"We could divide up the families among us," Matal suggested, his glance including the Huastecs in the circle. "Each of us could brief our group and start the process of getting everyone's agreement."

Matal was a natural leader, Caleb thought with approval. How quickly Matal had matured during the recent trials of the Huastecs! The other Huastec warriors already followed him willingly, and the challenges were only beginning.

"Is everyone in agreement with this approach?" Tonah asked.

Murmurs and nods of assent went around the assemblage.

"Then we must make haste. We will reconvene tomorrow night. If we have everyone's agreement, we must begin planning for the move to Kaibito's camp."

"What about the supplies; guns, ammunition, horses, carts?" Caleb added. "We have a lot to do to get ready."

"Leave that to us," Manuelito spoke up. "My men can use some of your silver to purchase guns and ammunition in Mexico. We will secure the carts and horses quietly among villages near our reservation."

Caleb shook his head quietly to himself. Somehow they must secure supplies and move over two hundred people over a hundred miles through the desert without being discovered. And they must do it all in little more than a week! It would take a miracle to pull it off.

Shanni stood up and faced the assembled men. "Many changes to our customary ways will be required. Anyone capable of fighting, man or woman, must be trained and equipped. We cannot anticipate all the dangers we will face, so each of the Huastecs must be ready to do their part. Be sure the families understand, for there can be no turning back. We must reach the Center of our ancestors or we will all die."

The men nodded, agreeing with Shanni's words. Their mood was somber as they got up to carry out their duties.

A week later, Lieutenant Porter and his soldier escort arrived with the Indian Agent at the Chaco River. They halted their horses to gaze across at the tents of the Navaho camp, scattered peacefully along the bank of the stream. Porter blinked, not believing his eyes. Nearly a hundred Huastec dwellings had disappeared as if they had never existed. Porter let out his breath and held his peace.

ANASAZI QUEST, third in the ANASAZI PRINCESS series is targeted for publication in December, 2002. Check www.pentaclespress.com for details.

Books by James Gibson:
at
www.pentaclespress.com

Anasazi Princess
Anasazi Journey

Order Form

To order additional copies, fill out this form and send it along with your check or money order to: James N. Gibson LLC, P.O. Box 51, Novi, MI 48376.
Or order online: www.pentaclespress.com

Cost per copy $9.95 plus $2.95 P&H. (MI residents add 6% sales tax)

Ship _____ copies of *Anasazi Journey* to:

Name_____

Address:_____

City:_____

State/Zip:_____

❏   Check box for signed copy